Reining Men
The Boot Knockers Ranch Series book 3
All Rights Reserved
Copyright Em Petrova 2017
Print Edition
Electronic book publication February 2017

There's no escaping ranch policy — anything to please a lady…

The Boot Knockers Ranch, Book 3

The Boot Knockers Ranch caters to women in all ways. And now rookie Paul is officially part of the team. He's had six months to hone his skills with the ladies and prides himself on being a prime catch.

Jack would agree. He can't get the rugged cowboy out of his system. He wants Paul in his bed more than anything, but his best friend has always been resistant to relations with other men. Jack's instinct says different, but he values Paul's friendship too highly to push it.

Then Jack takes on beautiful new client Lissy Lofton and finds himself falling hard for the confident show jumper. He's not the only one. Lissy has caught Paul's attention, and the attraction is mutual.

But now Jack has a problem. Lissy's sexual appetite is so ravenous, he doubts he can last the week without backup. Which presents an irresistible opportunity to invite Paul into their bed — where the incandescent heat brings all their walls tumbling down.

Warning: Contains two smoking-hot cowboys whose drive to please the same woman spurs a desire to please each other.

Dedication

Don't pee on the electric fence.

Reining Men

by

Em Petrova

Chapter One

Paul leaned against the gate, the pickup idling behind him. Up here on the ridge, it was hard to think about the ranch lazing in the afternoon heat in the valley below. Especially when he remembered what was really going on behind the closed doors of those bungalows dotting the land.

Sex, and plenty of it.

He scuffed his knuckles over his jaw, aware of the rasp. The ladies liked him rough around the edges, and he did his best to please.

"Here they come." Jack Iverwellar pushed away from the side of the truck, tugging his work gloves onto his hands.

Paul stuck his dark brown cowboy hat on his head, shielding his eyes from the sun. The big cattle truck crested the ridge, the lowing of the new livestock echoing across the prime Texas land.

"I'll get the gate." Jack strode over to it and jammed his fist into the bolt. It swung free, and he opened it all the way to allow the cattle truck entry.

Paul jumped behind the wheel of the pickup and waited for his buddy to get in. As his boot- and denim-clad leg appeared, Paul tapped the gas.

The truck lurched ahead.

Jack caught himself and jumped in just in time. His eyes creased with mirth. "Shithead."

"I'm paying you back for all the times you've done that to me." Grinning, Paul centered his attention on the dirt track leading around the ridge. He and Jack had spent countless hours up here building fence for the new additions to the herd. When the two of them weren't helping female clients with their sexual problems on The Boot Knockers Ranch, they were here, working toward a new venture.

The ranch was expanding. Recently they'd had an opportunity to buy more land, and Hugh, their leader and founder of the club, had jumped at the chance.

Paul was looking forward to this co-op he and Jack had forged. More cows, a prime breed known for perfectly marbled beef. They'd get a damn good price for them at auction. Besides the ranch's most important business—women—they were adding horses and cows. Hugh promised they'd be millionaires if they invested their dividends right.

Guiding the truck around to the spot of land he and Jack had prepared for the arrival of the cows, he glanced at his friend. Jack looked like a kid who'd just hit his first homerun.

"Feels good to finally see this day," Jack said, running his hands over his thighs.

"A good reward after all those sore muscles from pounding fence posts."

"If I recall, I swung the sledgehammer way more than you did."

Paul threw him a look. "Keep believing that, asshole."

"Do you think you're the only one who has ever worked hard for this ranch?"

"I was a ranch hand for years. I put in my time." He swept his hand, gesturing to the acres in the valley below. "Who do you think helped build all the bungalows so you could pop all those cherries?"

Jack's specialty was deflowering women. Girls who had hang-ups about men, thirty-year-old virgins and women with low self-esteem who just hadn't gotten the chance to be with a man—all paid big money for Jack's help.

Paul heard he was ultra-suave and tender with the women he slept with. He must be — he'd claimed dozens of cherries over the years. If only Paul felt as confident about his skills in bed.

Stowe was known as the Dom from Down Under; Booker was a master with sex toys. And until Damian had handed in his resignation, he'd been known as the rope king. Now he was busy tying his new wife up in knots — and they had a baby on the way.

Paul fulfilled a lot of women and heard no complaints. But he didn't yet know his specialty.

Jack punched Paul in the shoulder, and the muscle tightened under his friend's blow. "Every day I'm lying on my back while a beautiful woman rides me, I stare at the ceiling and thank you for building it."

Chest vibrating with laughter, Paul shook his head. "Sure you do."

"I'm dead serious. Those beams you built into the ceiling of Bungalow 4 are the strongest I've ever seen. Elliot pulled hard enough to bring the whole place down the other day when I tied him up for Collette. Your handiwork held."

4

A dark unease slithered into Paul's stomach. Jack had men pretty often. The ladies liked to break out of their shells with threesomes sometimes. And Jack made it known he loved cock as much as pussy.

Paul gazed out the window at the lazing ranch. Steam rose from the plush lawn, dew burning off in the morning sun. He stopped the truck and put it in park.

Jack was staring at him.

For a long minute Paul met his gaze. Jack had let it be known on several occasions that Paul would be his next conquest.

But Paul would never let that happen. He wasn't into guys. Especially one of his best friends.

"What?" he asked with a flat tone he hoped disguised his discomfort. How many times had he pushed Jack away? Told him to find another Boot Knocker to pursue?

Jack fisted his hand on his knee. "You never get used to me talking about fucking men, do you? Doesn't it turn you on just a little to know I lubed Elliot and slid in—"

"Shut up." Paul ripped open the door and jumped to the ground, watching the cattle truck roll toward them while visions of the sex

Jack described played through his head like some insane porn movie.

He set his hands on his hips and waited.

The passenger door slammed shut, and Jack joined him.

They were matched in height and build. Their senses of humor kept the strain out of their working relationship too. If not for being able to joke about Jack's constant pursuit, they would have fallen out long ago.

Sure, they'd had a few scuffles. When Jack couldn't keep his hands to himself, Paul drew his boundary.

It hadn't stopped Jack yet, though.

Jack shifted his weight, so close Paul could feel the man's heat down his side. When Jack brushed his knuckles against his, he jerked his hand away. He hurried to meet the driver.

"Randall, how the hell are you, man?" He shook hands with the crusty cattle broker, trying to erase Jack's touch.

An image jumped into Paul's mind — of Jack last night. The Boot Knockers held a weekly rodeo for the ladies, where they showed off their roping and riding skills. Jack had gotten a little out of control.

And a little nekkid.

With his leather vest hanging off one shoulder and his cowboy hat dangling from his erect cock, he'd gyrated while twirling an invisible rope.

Paul shook himself and focused on Randall.

"I'm good." He whistled through his teeth, looking around at the spread. "You've made a lot of improvements already. Old Murdoch would be proud to see his land made useful again."

"Yeah, I'm going to snap some photos and take them to him in the nursing home," Paul said.

Jack came forward and shook Randall's hand too. Paul noted the dry *swish* of their hands. Too well Paul knew how Jack's callused hands felt, since the man put them on him every chance he got. Sometimes it made his stomach weird.

He put another step of space between him and Jack.

"I'm ready to start offloading as soon as you are," Randall said.

Jack reached into the back of the pickup and gathered two coils of rope. He passed one to Paul as they positioned themselves at the rear of the truck. Randall opened the back, and they lowered a ramp.

The first heifer that stepped off the truck must have weighed a thousand pounds already. By the time they fattened her on grass and good minerals, she'd weigh as much as a bull.

A grin stretched across Jack's face. Paul let out a whoop, and they drifted together. Jack clasped his shoulder, and Paul clamped a hand over his friend's. He gave Jack a little shake, unable to contain the fever of excitement.

* * * * *

Jack's balls tightened as the fresh scents of man and soap filled his head. Paul was a fucking beautiful cowboy, and he pushed all the right buttons in Jack. Broad chest, carved ass. And his ice-blue eyes lanced right through Jack.

Too bad he didn't swing that way, because all the Elliots on the ranch wouldn't equal one heated roll in the hay with Paul.

Jack drank in the man's worn jeans and T-shirt with The Boot Knockers Ranch logo. Today he also wore a bandana knotted around his neck, and it was already darkened with sweat.

Sweat Jack wanted to lick off his skin.

Shit, he had it bad. For six months since Paul had been voted in as an official Boot Knocker, Jack had battled his cravings. His advances roused Paul's anger, so he tried to stomp on the sprouts of lust. Sometimes it was impossible.

Paul released his shoulder, but the skin still tingled from his touch. He forced himself to let go of Paul before he ended up yanking him into his hold and kissing the hell out of him.

Damn.

The hair on his forearms rose despite the eighty-degree weather and high humidity. He reluctantly moved away. As another handful of cows trotted off the truck, he spotted a spring calf. It was crowded against the metal slats of the truck, holding one leg up.

Before his mind wrapped around the danger of jumping into the truck with thousands of pounds of animals, Jack stepped onto the ramp. He made it two steps.

"Jack! What the hell are you doing?" Paul hollered.

His presence on the truck was spooking the cows. Snorting, stamping. One rushed past him. He kept going.

"Hey!" Randall called.

Paul ran around the side of the truck and gazed up between the slats. "What are you doing?"

"Hurt calf. I'm offloading them all faster," he grunted. He sent a few more trotting down the ramp then used his shoulder to move a heifer out of the way. He had to get them away from the baby, which cowered against the edge.

More cows made it off the truck, leaving a gap for Jack to safely maneuver. Crouching, he brought his arms around the calf's legs, folding them against his chest.

He used his thigh muscles to push into a stand, bearing the weight of the calf. He turned to the ramp once more.

Cows scattered, but one stubborn animal planted her hooves and refused to move.

"Paul!"

"Shit. Why couldn't you wait to get all the animals off?" Paul jogged to the head of the ramp and gathered his rope in his gloved fist.

Watching Paul swing the rope shouldn't be erotic, but it was to Jack.

He hitched the calf against his chest.

Paul threw the lasso. It fell in a perfect arc over the cow's head. As soon as it hit her neck, he yanked the rope. She issued a moo of dislike, but Paul tugged her forward.

Behind him, the other animals that hadn't been offloaded milled restlessly, slamming the sides of the truck and making it rock. The calf's muscles coiled, and Jack tightened his hold in case it tried to break free.

Paul was right. The animals should have come off first, but Jack hadn't been thinking about anything but saving the baby.

"C'mon, you stubborn heifer," Paul said through gritted teeth. He leaned into the rope, using his body weight to move the cow a few inches.

"Get lower. It will change your leverage," Jack called over the noise of too many cows stuck on a truck. If they stampeded, Jack and the calf would be trampled. And Paul would be forced to jump out of the way.

Except he was stubborn enough to keep trying to move the problem cow. He might not move in time.

"Give her foreleg a kick," Randall encouraged.

The older generation did things that way, but Jack didn't totally agree with it. Obviously Paul didn't either. Leaning back, he dug in his boots and used his weight and strength. The cow lurched forward a foot, the rope slackened and Paul's ass hit the ground.

He popped up with a grunt and a red face.

Jack's insides stirred at the sight. This was no time to feel aroused, but damn if he could help it. The flush on Paul's face, the way the vein ticked in his temple...hell, Jack wanted to bend him over and sink into his muscled body.

Again and again.

Randall darted forward and delivered a light kick to the cow's foreleg. It gave a loud moo and ambled down the ramp.

Paul caught the end of the rope and wrapped it around his fist several times, determination set on his rugged features. When he shot Jack a glance, the familiar need heated Jack's gut.

The cow ran the rest of the way down the ramp.

Jack was jostled from behind. Clinging to the hurt calf, he somehow got off the truck without being stomped by a cow. The feisty specimen Paul was wrangling was still giving him a fit.

"This one's going to take me for a ride!" Paul hooted, grinning.

Jack raised his jaw at Randall. "Lower the tailgate of the truck so I can put the calf in." The baby needed medical attention. It could have been crushed against the side during their journey. A weak animal meant predators would have a feast, and Jack couldn't let that happen.

As soon as he placed the calf in the truck, he shut the tailgate and went to lend a hand to Paul.

When he reached him, blood was trickling down his jaw. Jack sucked in a sharp breath. "What the hell happened to you?" He rushed forward, took the rope from his friend, and used the adrenaline coursing through his system to drag the stubborn-ass cow to the fencing.

He loosened the rope around its neck and then gave it a nudge with his boot. Turning back to Paul, he found blood dripping onto his friend's shirt.

In two strides he reached his friend. Gently he placed his fingers over the wound. Hot blood slicked his fingers.

Hissing, Paul jerked away. "Don't."

A hollow blossomed in Jack's chest, and an ache filled it. He didn't like seeing that blood or the crease of pain between Paul's brows.

"You need to get back to the ranch and let Holly see to you. How did it happen?"

"Damn thing shifted, and I hit the side of the truck." He fingered the ragged edge of the cut between his cheekbone and ear. "It's fine."

"You might need a tetanus shot."

Paul leveled him in his gaze, one light brown brow quirked. "Don't you remember two months ago? When we all lined up and the doc stuck a needle in our arms?"

Yeah, all twenty of them had gotten a mandatory physical including a tetanus booster. Hugh was a stickler about their care.

"Too bad it wasn't your ass. I woulda liked to have seen that."

Jack's joke achieved exactly what he wanted. The pain on Paul's face vanished, replaced by annoyance tinged with amusement. Shaking his head, Paul twisted away. "Let's get the last of the cows unloaded."

Together they worked side by side, shooing animals into the fencing. Jack roped another cow that proved not as stubborn as its fellow. As soon as Jack tugged the rope, the animal scurried into the pasture.

When every last beast was enclosed in the open expanse of grassland, Paul and Jack turned to Randall.

"You got the check from Hugh?" Jack asked.

"Yes, it arrived yesterday. I'll stop on my way out of the ranch to say hi. Nice doing business with you. Good luck with your venture." Randall pushed the chewing tobacco into his cheek and shook their hands again.

Randall climbed into his truck and guided it back down the ridge. Hitching a thumb in his jeans, Jack turned to watch the milling herd.

Paul leaned his elbows on the fence, ignoring the cut. "Well, that was definitely a change from finessing women."

"I don't know. Sometimes I think the cows require more finesse than the women."

Paul burst out laughing, his eyes softening. Jack moved to stand beside his friend. This time when he stood too close, Paul didn't move away. They stared at the cows that would butter their bread a little more. By the time they were too old to keep their cocks up all day and night, they'd have enough money to retire.

"Do you like the stud ranch part of your job, Paul?"

He started. When their gazes met, Jack's breath hitched. Hell, he wished he could either convince Paul to let him in — all the way — or he wished he could quit having these feelings.

Paul sniffed. "'Course I like it. Helping beautiful women fulfill their dreams? What's not to love?"

"I don't know. Do you ever feel there's something missing?"

When Paul pivoted to face him, Jack's body responded. Want speared him. His cock jolted, growing instantly. He ran his tongue over his lower lip.

"What do you mean?" Paul asked.

What *did* he mean? Damn, he was getting all sappy over a bit of blood oozing from a cut on his buddy's face.

"Never mind. Let's get the calf back to the barn. Now that last week's ladies are gone, we won't have to rip Quay from between a

16

woman's legs. He's the best with animals. He'll be able to fix up the calf." Taking a chance, Jack lightly touched Paul's cheek, just above the cut.

This time when Paul jerked away, he was prepared. It still hurt like hell, though.

* * * * *

The hot sand burned the soles of Lissy's bare feet, and the sun burned the bridge of her nose. She needed to apply more sunscreen, but not now — not while the score was 11-9.

The volleyball sailed right toward her. She planted her feet and extended her arms. When the ball launched off her forearms right to her partner, she held her breath. Melia was the best spiker on the regional team, and she rarely missed a shot.

As the ball spiked right into the ground in front of the opposing two-player team, the fans on the sidelines went wild.

Melia whirled toward Lissy, her face wild with joy. She jumped into Lissy's arms and they did a victory dance.

They pulled apart, sweat slicking both their bodies.

The other team was setting up to serve again. Lissy ran to the back of the sand pit and readied herself. Her hair dripped into her eye, having escaped her high ponytail, and she shoved it back.

And then she was running, bouncing all over the court, setting up Melia for a spike she missed.

The opposite team got a point.

"Sorry," Melia said, panting from exertion.

"It's okay. We'll get the next one."

The tournament had been going on for three hours. Team Lofton-Moore was the team to beat, according to the pro volleyball players commentating for the televised event.

During her rest time, Lissy had heard them talking about the "Double L and M team"— Lissy Lofton and Melia Moore. People were placing bets on their win, and that put even more pressure on Lissy. She wasn't as dedicated to the sport as Melia was, and her partner wanted this win. Lissy's passion was horse jumping. In fact, she'd been so engulfed in it that she had left little time for things like men.

"Lissy!" Melia called, snapping her back to the game.

She dug in, thigh muscles burning, her toes spread to give her better purchase in the sand. When she dived, the ball struck squarely on her arms and arced over the net. In a flash, she was on her feet, sand clinging to her bare torso, her spandex boy shorts riding up her crack.

No time to pick them out—the ball was sailing her direction again.

"Shit." She lunged again, mouth full of sand, a grain in her left eye. Melia almost toppled on her as she hurled herself forward in time to keep the ball from hitting the ground.

The fans erupted with applause.

Melia stuck out a hand, and Lissy grabbed it, letting her teammate pull her up. She gained her wits in time to send the ball back across the net.

Her muscles hummed with power. All her life she'd been athletic—basketball, volleyball, track. She'd even joined the girls' martial arts class for a spell in fifth grade. But the first time she'd seated a horse, she felt everything click into place.

Melia's boyfriend stood on the sidelines, grinning, and a seed of jealousy sprouted in

Lissy. Whether they won this match or not, her friend would walk into his arms afterward. Lissy wanted that.

The fans were chanting her name as she barreled toward the net, hell-bent on reaching the ball. Melia's dark hair tumbled out of the bun she'd anchored on top of her head, spilling over her shoulders.

The whistle blew as the ball went out of play. The girls took a few moments to brush sand out of places where sand should never be. Melia came close to whisper, "You're doing great. Good shut-outs. Keep it going."

Lissy held up a fist, and Melia bumped knuckles with her. They shared a grin.

The whistle shrilled, and they were at it again. Running, volleying, spiking. Melia hit her knees to get a ball, and Lissy almost careened into her. Somehow they kept the game going.

Waves crashed on the shore, and while she was killing herself on the volleyball court, others were picnicking on the beach with their families. Would she ever be in their place?

One thing was certain. She wasn't going to meet men on a woman's volleyball circuit. And she needed to get rid of the little obstacle known as virginity. As soon as she finished this tour, she'd focus on herself.

If she got rid of her cherry, she would feel lighter; she knew it. She might have the drive to find that perfect man who filled the hole in her heart the way horse riding and sports had always completed her before.

She'd been too focused on her pursuits, and that hadn't included a man.

"Get it, Lissy!"

"Lofton, Lofton!"

She raced forward, kicking up sand. The ball was a white orb flying at her, silhouetted by the blazing California sun. She connected.

The ball flew straight up, up, up.

And Melia came at it with that deadly accurate blow—the one that sent the volleyball into the sand, earning a win for Team Double L-M.

Chapter Two

Paul paused in the doorway of the bunkhouse. Poker playoffs—he'd forgotten. The guys had set up tables and cigar smoke hung in the air. Between batches of clients, the Boot Knockers kicked back with a game of cards, beer and usually a practical joke or two.

He scanned the room, and Jack caught his gaze.

"Here's a seat." Jack kicked the chair leg, and it scooted away from the table. Paul maneuvered his way through the group to take a seat beside his friend. Had Jack saved it for him?

He spun the chair and straddled it. "It's damn hot in here." Sweat snaked down his spine, making his Western shirt cling to his skin. Using his knuckles, he nudged his hat up to peer at the table.

"We'll deal you in next hand," Jack said.

Since he wasn't playing, Paul took the liberty to inspect first Ty's hand then Jack's. Jack leaned in, displaying the cards freely.

Paul pointed and Jack nodded. No one cared if Jack got Paul's opinion on what to play. When you were playing for sunflower seeds, the stakes weren't too high.

"You two finished being an old married couple?" Elliot asked.

"You're the one spending the night with him," Paul responded.

Paul flicked one of the sunflower seeds from the pile in the center at the dark-haired man with the thick Southern drawl. He was a title holder in rodeo team roping and bore a belt buckle tattoo on his forearm, which he showed off almost as much as the actual buckle holding up his jeans.

The ladies melted into puddles at the sight of an authentic rodeo cowboy.

While the guys burst into laughter, Paul got up and circled the table to the beer cooler. He snagged two and returned to his seat.

For a minute he chewed his lip, trying to decide how he felt about Elliot's barb. Since Hugh had fallen for his best friend, Riggs, the guys were ultra-aware of friendships. Some of them had been teasing each other, saying they were "pulling a Riggs," but it was all in good fun.

From the corner of his eye, he found Jack's gaze on him. That muscle in the crease of his jaw was fluttering. Was he pissed off that Paul had mentioned his roping with Elliot?

Paul slid a beer toward his friend. Jack curled his fingers around the dewy bottle, the tips brushing Paul's. Careful not to jerk away and give the guys another reason to tease them, he sat back and watched the game.

The adjoining table was getting rowdier by the second, the voices rising and rising again.

The people at Paul's table twisted to see what was going on. Booker lunged across the table. Shoulders separated, and Paul glimpsed a long black dildo lying across their sunflower seed pile.

He burst into laughter.

"Are they betting horse dongs over there?" Jack asked. The guys at their table shook with laughter.

Paul tipped back to speak to Jeremy. "What's going on?"

Jeremy's grin was wide and infectious. "Quay's idea. Best of five hands gets the black dick toy."

Overhearing, Booker narrowed his eyes. "Oh, I'll win. I've been looking for one for my collection." Booker's toy collection was notorious and took up a massive cupboard. It was shocking he didn't yet have the rubbery specimen lying on the table.

More raucous laughter, and Paul hid his smile by sipping his beer. Jack made a play and Elliot folded. Finn followed. That left Jack and Blake.

No way would Blake concede defeat even if he was holding junk cards. He was hot-headed and would fight hard for almost everything. Each week when they'd argue to determine who would be whose personal Boot Knocker, no one wanted to go against Blake.

Actually, Paul had only seen Blake lose to one person—Damian.

Someone fired up another cigar, and the rich smoke filtered into Paul's head. He hadn't smoked in a long time, and suddenly it sounded good.

"Hey, Stowe. You have a cigar on you?"

"Yeah, mate." No matter how many years the Australian cowboy spent in Texas, he never lost his accent. He fished in his breast pocket and came out with a cigar.

Paul accepted it with a grunt and lit it with the lighter he always carried. As a former Boy Scout, he came prepared with pocket knife and windproof lighter. While The Boot Knockers

Ranch wasn't exactly a wilderness, one couldn't be too careful while working outdoors.

He leaned against the chair back and smoked and watched the game.

Was it his imagination or did Jack keep throwing glances at Elliot?

"I raise you twenty seeds," Jack drawled.

Paul got up and went around the table to look at Blake's hand.

"Hey! No cheating!" Blake's eyes practically turned red with anger. Damn, he really was competitive.

"He's not playing," Jack taunted.

"No, but he'll tell you what cards I'm holding."

Well, he hadn't intended to help Jack win, but now he would. He met Jack's gaze over Blake's shoulder. "Better make it forty seeds."

Jack's teeth flashed white in his tanned face. "Fifty seeds."

"Jesus, Hawkins, why would you tell him that?" Blake tossed down his cards, bowing out of the game.

Jack carefully laid his cards down and scooped a pile of seeds his direction. Elliot gave a whoop and clamped a hand on Jack's shoulder in congratulations.

Stomach filled with a weird flutter at the affectionate gesture between them, Paul looked away.

What the guys did in their own time was none of his business. He'd once picked on Riggs for his relations with Hugh, but he'd since realized how wrong he'd been. He hadn't just picked on Riggs — they'd gotten into several fistfights. Since becoming friends with Jack, Paul realized he didn't need to feign some uber-masculinity by mocking guys who slept with other men. It didn't affect him who somebody else slept with. In the end, Riggs had accepted his apology, and they were tentative friends now.

Blake gathered all the cards and made a show of shuffling, running the cards up his arm and flipping them as if they were dominoes.

"Where'd you learn to deal?"

"Had a stint in Vegas when I was twenty." He manipulated the cards into an arc. They spilled into his open palm like a waterfall.

"Bet that was a wild ride," Elliot said.

"Not as wild as being a Boot Knocker." Blake started tossing them cards, his hands moving so fast they were a blur.

"Have any of you looked at the files for this week's batch of women?" Jeremy asked. He was one of the youngest on the ranch, but the years he'd spent in the sun had hardened him enough that the older ladies weren't put off by a baby face.

"Nah, I quit looking."

"Me too."

"I looked." Jack's voice sounded odd. Strained.

"Too goddamn hot in here." Jack pushed off his hat and half stood to peel off his T-shirt. The carved lines of his back glistened with sweat, and the dark blond strands of hair on his nape were damp.

He plunked into the seat again and resumed the faceoff against Blake.

Elliot was staring at Jack's chest. The man had double nipple piercings, and he claimed the small gold hoops heightened sensation during sex. For a short time Paul had kicked around the idea of having his pierced, but his traditional leanings had kept him out of the

28

piercing parlor. "Good idea, bro." Elliot stood and took his time stripping off his shirt too.

"A mite cooler," Jack said, staring at Elliot.

Gnawing his lip, Paul picked up his cards. God, what a shitty hand. The best he could hope for was to stay in the game until he couldn't bluff his way through anymore.

He stubbed out his cigar and finished his beer. Jack leaned back in his chair, thighs falling open. Paul's gaze was directed to the bulge between them.

He tossed down his cards. "I'm done. Gotta get some air."

* * * * *

As Paul left the table, Jack's skin prickled with awareness. Why the hell had he fallen for a guy who was a homophobe?

From a young age, Jack had recognized his attraction to both sexes. To him, there was no difference in genders. If he ever settled down, he didn't care if it was with a man or woman. To him, love was love.

Not that he'd ever been in love. Lust, yeah. He wanted to grip Paul's square jaw and plunge his tongue into his mouth. Then he wanted to guide Paul down his body to suck his cock.

His boxers grew uncomfortably tight, and oh yeah, Elliot was looking. Tonight Jack would probably take the muscled cowboy to bed, but that wouldn't keep his thoughts from Paul—and Lissy.

He'd looked at the files, and one girl had caught his attention—and held it. He'd stared at her smiling photograph, searching the lights in her eyes and wondering how someone who looked so happy and carefree could possibly have trouble with her sex life.

Before he'd even read her file, he'd made up his mind to fight for her. Then he saw it— the V word. Virgin. She had a cherry to steal, and he *was* the virgin slayer.

His balls clenched tight to his body, his shaft distended. He took a long swallow of his beer and played the game. Under the table, Elliot nudged his knee.

Jack loved getting into bed with Elliot. He'd made the man scream out two releases before he'd let him out of the ropes. Then Elliot had been soft and pliant, willing to take anything Jack had to give. Which was a nice, long pounding in the ass.

All the while visions of Paul had kept popping up.

Elliot leaned close, his mouth at Jack's ear. "Want to play tonight?"

Did he?

Paul appeared suddenly, and Jack straightened away from Elliot. "Better not. Save it for the ladies tomorrow."

As Paul straddled his chair again, Jack gave him a sidelong look. His cock throbbed.

The games went on. Booker did not win the dildo up for grabs, and another cowboy they called Montana pushed away from the table and walked out of the bunkhouse, the dildo resting on his shoulder.

* * * * *

"I think I'll call it a night," Paul said.

"How do you plan to go to bed when the games are going on?" Jack gestured to the row of bunks lining the wall. When the women came, the bunkhouse was pretty empty. The guys slept with their ladies if they desired. And most did.

"Think I'll grab my roll and head up to the ridge, sleep up there with the cows." Paul's eyes were dead serious, a sea of calm blue.

Jack's breath hitched. "Want some company?"

Paul went dead still. So much innuendo in that question, and yet it wasn't strange at all when they shared the duty of the herd. Since the animals had just been dumped onto the ranch that morning, it wasn't unusual for them to get spooked or some to fall ill.

Besides, they had to keep an eye out for predators running that ridge. It would be smart to head up there with a shotgun and some ammo.

Paul gave a jerky nod. "Sure. I don't care what you get up to in the meantime. Just make sure you're wearing pants when you get to the ridge."

Blake guffawed, and Elliot looked relieved.

Jack needed to put some distance between him and Elliot. He wasn't in the market for a full-time lover, and he didn't need the stress of a jealous boy toy.

He swallowed the rest of his beer and set the bottle on the table with a *clink*. "I'll meet you up there."

Without a word, Paul headed toward his bunk. He gathered his bedroll and left the building.

Hugh's booming voice rang out from the doorway. "A fresh crop of girls on the ranch tomorrow. Early lights-out. I think you'll find some feisty ones in the group. And remember, when they're onstage, keep your hands in your lap and your—"

"Peckers in your pants," they all chorused.

Hugh gave a crooked grin. "That's right, Boot Knockers. See you in the auditorium tomorrow."

Jack wrapped up his poker game and got dressed. Feeling a little nervous at being alone with a guy who didn't want the same things Jack did, he grabbed his bedroll and headed to the ATV shed. He expected Paul to walk all that distance, but he was more of a four-wheeler kind of guy.

What was it about Paul that just did it for him? Besides being his best friend, the guy was fucking hot as hell. Carved abs, broad shoulders. He'd never seen Paul totally naked, but he could guess from the size of his bulge that he had enough to keep Jack happy.

Grabbing a key from a nail, he shook himself. Going there mentally would only cause a lot of torment tonight. Paul would be so close to him, yet they might as well be standing on opposite sides of the Grand Canyon when it came to their desires.

That word launched him into a new fixation—Lissy.

Her file held everything Jack needed to know. Five-feet, ten inches, long brown hair. She had a toothpaste-ad smile and long lashes. In her photo, she'd been wearing activewear, making it easy to picture her shooting hoops or even surfing. She was a California girl, after all.

While Holly and the production manager Isabel spent hours perusing the files and matching women with cowboys, in the end, the women chose. They browsed the Boot Knockers' photographs and chose the ones they were attracted to. Just because Jack was the best at soothing virgins, it didn't necessarily mean Lissy would want him.

Damn, what if she chose Blake? Stowe? No, he couldn't picture her with a Dom. He didn't know her personality, but after years of doing this job, he was pretty good at drawing conclusions from the files.

In the dark shed, he located a four-wheeler and tucked his bedroll on the back. Then he fired up the steel horse and took off across the fields. Feeling the horsepower between his legs was almost as much of a rush as riding a flesh-and-blood horse.

The breeze lifted the brim of his hat, threatening to tear it off his head. He pressed on the crown and held it in place as he zoomed up the hill. He couldn't stop thinking of Paul's expression when he'd stripped his shirt off earlier. He'd taken off his shirt plenty of times while working with Paul, but something was different in his expression tonight.

Maybe Paul's disapproval had swelled—maybe Jack had taken things too far. But he was an exhibitionist. Still, he couldn't help but wonder if he was less bold, more modest...

The moon rode high in the sky, a sliver providing little light. As Jack crested the ridge and hit the flat ground, Paul unfolded himself from the ground and stood. Jack's stomach clenched, his body responding to his friend's shadowed outline.

If he ever got Paul in his bed, his mind would be blown. By dawn he'd be a gibbering idiot.

Jack cut the engine and swung his leg off the ATV. As he approached, he saw something was very wrong with Paul.

"Is it the herd? Did we lose one?" he asked.

Paul slashed a hand through the air. "No, they're all okay. The hurt calf is still in the barn, being nursed by bottle until her leg heals."

"It was broken?" Unable to stop himself, Jack moved closer to Paul. The sound of crickets and the fresh scent of grass enclosed them in a private cocoon.

Drawing a deep breath through his nose, Jack made out Paul's spicy scent.

"Not broken, just sprained. The vet fixed it up and said to keep the calf out of the field for a few days."

"What's wrong, man?"

"I'm not on the roster this week."

Jack released a low whistle and rubbed the back of his neck. Not a single cowboy on the ranch liked being the odd man out. Hugh liked to give each guy a rotating week off, but they all despised the downtime. When Jack had last been without a lady, he'd thought he'd die of blue balls.

In the end, Jeremy had invited him for a threesome, and he'd gotten a night of relief. But Jack really just hated sleeping alone.

"Sorry to hear that, Paul."

He kicked at a tuft of grass and nodded. "I can hang out with the herd."

"You're always welcome to hang out with me."

Again Paul hesitated, as he had during the poker game when Jack had slipped and said something hinting at his attraction.

"I didn't mean it like that. For once I'm not flirting. We're friends."

Silence stretched. Paul lowered himself to the ground and slung an arm around his knee. "I don't want to be a third wheel with you and a client."

Pushing out a breath, Jack sat too. The grass was dry and crackled under his jeans. "I respect your boundaries."

Paul stared at him for a long minute, his face incredulous. Then they both burst out laughing.

"Okay, so I don't respect your boundaries. But I *know* about them."

Paul's shoulders shook with laughter. "As long as we're clear on that."

They stared over the pasture for a while, the silence easier now.

"A hundred head of cattle looks a lot bigger in person than on paper," Paul said finally.

"That's for sure." Jack reached into his back pocket and pulled out a flask. It glinted silver in the moonlight. "Whiskey?"

"Yeah." Paul accepted it and swigged.

"Hey, take it easy. It's all I've got."

"After Holly told me I was off the roster this week, I detoured to the grub house and grabbed a whole bottle." Paul pointed at his belongings lying several feet away.

Jack waved a hand. "Help yourself then." Getting sloshed with the best buddy you wanted to land in bed with wasn't such a bad idea.

Paul raised the flask to his lips. Finding it empty, he tipped it over and shook a single drop from it. It landed on his wrist, caught in the hairs there.

Jack licked his lips, wanting more than anything to raise his wrist to his mouth and taste that drop of alcohol on his tongue. With any luck, Paul would let him—

No, he wouldn't.

He crawled on his hands and knees to retrieve the bottle Paul had brought.

"You can't get drunk," Paul warned. "You'll be hungover for your client."

Jack lifted a shoulder in a shrug and crawled back to where Paul sat. As he neared, Paul rested back, his arm folded beneath his head. His hat fell off, revealing mussed hair.

Jack's fingers twitched with the urge to run his fingers through it.

Unrequited lust was bad, but it was worsened by the fact they were friends. At every turn, Paul was there, tormenting him.

He took a long swallow of whiskey, ignoring the burn and focusing on how it made him feel a little less controlled.

Maybe it would do the same for Paul. He stuck out the bottle. Paul rolled onto his side and propped himself on an elbow in order to drink.

"Cooler out here than in the bunkhouse. It was a good idea to come to the pasture." Jack watched Paul's throat move as he swallowed. God, to see him swallowing something else.

In a blink, his cock swelled to full hardness.

Could it be that Jack was only smitten with his friend because Paul wasn't interested? Was it the chase that was stealing his goddamn mind?

Then Paul began to talk, and Jack threw himself down on his back and stared at the stars. No, it wasn't the hunt. It was Paul—period.

"This week will be hella uncomfortable without a woman."

Need stabbed low in Jack's groin.

"That last one…whooee. She was a wildcat once I got her uptight panties off. Low self-esteem? Pfaww…" He swigged. "She just needed a tender touch and a good listener. As far as I could tell, not one of her lovers had ever responded to her needs. She really needed three fingers. High and tight."

Paul held up three fingers, and Jack's cock lengthened another fraction. What he wouldn't give to watch Paul in action.

His friend wasn't usually into sharing, which meant the alcohol was freeing his tongue. They talked and drank and watched the cows. Jack confided a little about his dad down in Oklahoma being sick, and how he needed to take his week off to visit him.

"You need to do that." Paul said. "It's good you can take off and see your dad. Mine don't want me around."

Jack looked at him more closely. "Why not?"

"My brother turned them on me. He claimed I was a money-grubber, trying to get their estate after they were gone. But all I'd suggested was that my parents have a will. Things like that need to be spelled out when you reach a certain age."

"I agree. So what happened?"

"Mark filled their brains with poison and my parents stopped talking to me. It took me a while to figure out I should go my separate way and forget about having family ties. But lemme tell you, it hurt."

Paul's voice cracked. Jack couldn't stand it anymore.

He sat up and scooted the two feet of space between them. Then he cupped Paul's jaw, his thumb at the corner of his friend's mouth, burning to kiss him.

Paul stilled, every inch of his body hardening until he was strung as tight as a noose around a cattle thief's neck. "Jack." The word was a warning—a shot slicing through the night, and through Jack's heart.

He let his hand drop. "I'm sorry. I don't know why I do this. Too much whiskey I guess."

"Well, maybe that's enough alcohol." Paul got up and wandered to the fence. He rested his arms on the top and stared at the herd. Most cows were sleeping, huddled together. A plaintive moo sounded from the back corner.

Jack gazed at his back for a long time. He couldn't blame his actions on alcohol consumption, not when he'd gladly take Paul totally sober. Paul knew it, but he was trying to explain Jack's feelings away.

It pissed Jack off.

He got to his feet and strode to the fence. He should be subtle and keep the peace between them, but he was sick and tired of hiding his feelings..

Gripping Paul's shoulder, he swung him around.

And kissed him.

The first bruising crush of lips ignited him.

Paul's mouth worked into a snarl, and he shoved Jack away, hard. He stumbled a few steps and came right back at him. Clamping his hands around Paul's face, he leaned in and claimed his mouth.

Steely body flush against Jack's, the flavor of man and leather and a blade of grass he'd chewed.

God, it was so much better than he'd ever dreamed. Jack's cock ached, and he rocked his hips.

Paul jammed the heels of his hands into Jack's chest and shoved him. He lost his footing and his ass hit the ground. His teeth cracked together.

When Paul loomed over him, he expected a kick to the ribs or a fist in the jaw.

But Paul stuck out a hand. Jack took it, and he launched him to his feet. Without looking at him, Paul returned to the fence. "You've had too much alcohol."

"You know damn well I haven't."

"I'm not going to be one of your cherries, Jack."

"It's not like that." Jack's throat closed off. Damn, the whiskey was making him sappy now. The last thing he wanted when coming onto a guy was to sound whiney.

Damn, he could still taste traces of the cigar Paul had smoked. He ran his tongue over the roof of his mouth, savoring it.

"I value you as a friend. Don't take that away from me." Paul's stare unhinged Jack.

Right, friends. If he didn't have Paul in his bed, his hard body against his night after night, he had a good friend. He couldn't help but believe Paul was denying something, even to himself.

Pressing his lips into a line, he nodded. "Friends."

* * * * *

A petite brunette peeked at the girls in the waiting room. "Lissy?"

Nerves jangling, Lissy stood and moved toward the door. Ten other girls watched her, which made her more uneasy. She'd traveled onto The Boot Knockers Ranch with two of them. They'd been like the Three Amigos until this point.

Now Lissy was on her own, about to be quizzed about her sexual preferences and what she found attractive.

When she'd booked this trip to the ranch, she'd been on a high from that tournament win.

What Lissy had really come to terms with, though, was her life needed to change. So she'd taken control and decided to eliminate the problem of no sex life. If a week romping with a hot man in worn jeans and a cowboy hat didn't spur her to take time for a relationship, nothing would.

"I'm Holly, the office assistant here at the ranch. I'll be walking you through the procedure today and also asking some questions. Please have a seat."

The chair was purple velvet, seeming more at place on a porn movie set than an office. Once Lissy sank into it, she bit off a groan. After sitting on a plane for hours then a cab ride to the heart of Texas, the cushion felt like a cloud.

Holly's eyes sparkled. "Comfy, isn't it?"

"Yes." Lissy smiled.

"So, welcome. Our ranch is now three hundred acres of prime grazing land, and I think you'll find the cowboys are prime too." She winked, and Lissy caught her excitement. "You've looked over our brochure."

"Yes."

Let the Boot Knockers fulfill your wildest fantasies while showing you just how beautiful you really are.

She wasn't one of those girls who believed she wasn't attractive or worthy of a relationship. She just wanted the wildest fantasy part.

"I'm sure you spent some time looking at the cowboys on the cover."

Actually, she'd ogled those tanned, muscular chests for hours. Finally, she'd gotten so worked up, she'd slipped her fingers into her panties and given herself a toe-curling orgasm.

One cowboy stuck out to her, though.

The set of his jaw and the way he stood, one thumb hitched in his jeans pocket, had really gotten her juices flowing.

Holly slid a big photo album across the desk toward her. "I'd like you to look at these pictures and point out the guys you are attracted to."

Heart drumming a staccato beat, Lissy opened the cover. The first glossy photograph was a hunk. His windswept hair, line bracketing his mouth, both yelled *yeehaw*. She turned the page and found more pictures of him—with a horse, holding a rope, and from behind.

Ohhhh yeah.

She pressed her knees together.

Three more pages and she felt like a little kid browsing a toy catalog. She would choose her plaything, and the big fee she'd paid up front would put that toy in her hands.

When she turned another page, she stopped breathing.

It was him.

His gorgeous blue-green eyes were piercing on the page. In person, would she even be able to stare into eyes like that? Her nipples puckered under her tank top and she was grateful for her thick sports bra. She didn't want Holly to see her reaction.

But when she lifted her gaze, Holly was smiling.

"Forgive me, but I've done this job long enough to recognize the signs. Would you like me to put Jack down as one of your choices?"

Jack. *Oh my God, yes.*

Lissy pressed her fingertips to her lips and turned the page. Jack tossing a bale of hay, his shoulder muscles rippling. Jack kicked back in an Adirondack chair, a bottle of beer in his hand and his mouth relaxed in a smile. Jack without a cowboy hat, his thick hair ruffled in the wind.

She shut the album. "Yes, please put down Jack."

Holly chuckled. "Well, we'd like you to choose at least three cowboys from the book."

"Oh." Disappointment doused her desire. "Okay." She opened the album again and turned pages while Holly wrote Jack's name in a neat hand on a sheet of paper.

Every cowboy in the book was amazing. Magazine-ad material. One older guy with a wicked black beard could have been on the cover of *GQ*. All were buff and looked athletic, which was important to Lissy. She valued fitness and appreciated the hard work that went into the bodies on those pages.

When she reached the last page, she stopped. The man there was breathtaking. Ice-blue eyes, a scruff of beard glinting blond in the sun. He squinted, and small creases around his eyes only added to his allure.

The next photos were as arousing as his headshot.

"He's pretty," Lissy breathed.

Holly laughed. "Paul is a very beautiful man. Looks a little like that actor, don't you think?"

Lissy nodded.

"Good choices. I know you'll be satisfied with your cowboy. While we like our clients to make choices based on attraction, things sometimes work out a little differently. But rest assured our cowboys know how to do their jobs and you'll leave very satisfied. Now Isabel will take you backstage, where you will wait with the other ladies. When you're called onto the stage, the Boot Knockers will ask you questions. Often several of them fight over the lucky ladies. But in the end, it's your choice."

Lissy released a shaky breath. This was it. Countless solo orgasms would finally be shadowed by her first sexual encounter with a man. Why had she waited so long to get to this point in her life?

A door behind the desk opened, and another woman wearing wire-rimmed glasses entered. "Ready?"

"All set," Holly said, twisting in her leather chair. She and Lissy stood. "This is Lissy. Best of luck and enjoy your stay," she said to her.

Feeling as if her agility had fled, Lissy followed Isabel woodenly out the door and down a series of corridors. The final door opened onto blinding sunshine. Heat blasted her.

"Just this way." Isabel was quite a bit shorter than Lissy, as a lot of women were, but she had an air of confidence that made her seem bigger than she was. "These are the bungalows." She waved a hand at the small buildings with red roofs. "Over there is the grub house. Or the dining hall, as some call it."

"I bet the cowboys don't call it the dining hall."

Isabel laughed. "No, they don't. And here is the auditorium. Follow me."

They went into a dark, cool space. It took a moment for Lissy's eyes to adjust—in time to spot the other girls gathered in a knot, talking. Isabel gestured for Lissy to join them, then disappeared again, obviously making the walk back to Holly's office to retrieve another victim.

Er—client.

Lissy was good at making small talk with strangers, but her pulse was a constant thrum in her skull. She felt the first inklings of a headache, which she often suffered from when stressed. She massaged her temples and tried to calm herself.

What she hoped to get from this trip was a few amazing orgasms at the hands of a gorgeous cowboy. It wasn't a traditional way to reach her end goal, but she was sick of playing by the rules.

The rule book wasn't working for her.

She talked to a woman with legs a mile long and found out she wasn't the only virgin backstage.

Feeling a little easier in her skin, Lissy drew a deep breath and tried to trample her nervousness. That worked for all of twenty minutes, when Isabel called her name and Lissy stepped into the spotlight.

Chapter Three

Jack bounced on the toes of his cowboy boots, burning to go backstage and see if Lissy was everything in person that she was on paper. Since setting eyes on that little photograph, he'd felt almost as off-balance as the times he was around Paul.

The auditorium was dim, two lines of plush leather chairs under spotlights and the buttons glowing red in front of them. Within minutes he'd push his for Lissy — and he'd win her, dammit. He couldn't let another cowboy lay hands on her.

He rubbed his palms together and watched the other guys file in. Hugh led the group with Riggs right behind, looking at his lover's ass.

Jack shook himself. Right now he had to focus on Lissy.

Holly stood on the sidelines, a stack of folders in hand. As the Boot Knockers took their seats, she began to pass them out. Each man had his assignment before the fists started striking buttons, but sometimes things didn't play out perfectly. The fake fights sometimes were very real. Sometimes a cowboy wouldn't back down. Assignments were well and good, but they were red-blooded men. If one of them saw an opportunity to get what he wanted, he'd take it. That meant switching up several assignments, but the cowboys didn't mind. They loved helping women.

If anyone challenged him, Jack would fight for Lissy.

He'd started to drift to his chair when he spotted Paul. He stood at the back of the auditorium, arms folded, hat pushed back enough for Jack to make out his features.

His chest grew tight. Sheesh. What the hell was the matter with him? Maybe he really was a randy goat. Sleeping with the other guys, hungering after Paul and harboring a protective streak for a girl whose picture he'd only seen a few times.

Paul raised two fingers in a sort of wave, and Jack took his seat. As soon as his ass touched leather, his nerves kicked in.

He bounced his foot and leaned forward, waiting for Holly to bring the files. As she moved down the line, the guys flirted and exchanged banter with her. She was as cute as a button—and also gay. She wouldn't even swing a little bit from her path—every Boot Knocker had tried at least twice.

Jack a few more times than that.

Damn, was he a cowboy slut? What was wrong with him?

When Holly set the folders in front of him, he flipped through until he found the only one he wanted.

Ahhhh, yes.

Lissy Lofton. Sparkling eyes, amazing smile. And a virgin.

Not for long.

He set her file off to the side and didn't bother glancing at the others. He'd put on a good show by pushing a button for someone else's client, but he wouldn't try too hard to win.

When he glanced over his shoulder, Paul had pulled away from the wall and taken a seat at the back of the auditorium with Sybill. The woman who had shaken the dynamics of The Boot Knockers Ranch sat with legs crossed and a big smile on her pretty face. Hugh and Riggs had gone crazy for her, and when they refused to give her up, they stepped down. Now they lived in a bungalow made for three.

As Paul talked, he waved a hand in the air, the chunky gold ring on his finger glinting.

Jack had spent enough time studying everything about Paul that he knew him right down to that elk-tooth ring. He'd picked it up north in Cody during his last week off.

Maybe Paul would leave the ranch and explore again this week.

Pivoting to face forward again, Jack glanced at Lissy's name. It sounded good. Felt good on his tongue. He just had a feeling about this one — she wouldn't be the stereotypical shy virgin.

No, that gleam in her eyes was too vibrant for her to be anything but fun-loving and outgoing.

Hugh walked down the line of cowboys, hands clasped behind his back. "Remember, Boot Knockers, give them a good show. Make them feel desired before they even get off that stage, and do your best all week to fulfill their dreams so they can leave here with a new outlook on life. That's our goal. Understand?"

Of course they did. They'd been listening to Hugh's spiel every week for years and years. Jack enjoyed the selection process now as much as he had the very first time. He loved women.

And men.

He glanced at Paul, who smiled at him.

The heaviness in Jack's groin grew. All night long he'd fantasized about curling up behind Paul on that ridge and kissing his neck while taking him in the ass, nice and slow. He'd tried to jerk off in the wee hours of the morning, but Paul had roused at the rustling noise.

That meant Jack was still loaded and ready to go.

Hopefully Lissy wouldn't need a slow hand.

What was he thinking? Of course she would.

"Keep your hands in your laps and your peckers in your pants!" Hugh said, and some of the guys chorused with him.

Jack needed to move, bad. Anxiety spread through his system like ants at a picnic.

The first woman took the stage—tall, slender, her dark hair cropped short and her hands twisting. The spotlight highlighted the sun-kissed streaks in her hair and the sunburn on the tip of her nose.

To give his hands something to do, he found her file and opened it. Jessie Garraty. Thirty-one years old, native of Tallahassee.

Occupation: travel agent. She had trouble with body image—a history of anorexia, though she looked healthy now.

He closed the file. She was Booker's type for sure. He'd work wonders with her, pumping up her self-esteem while wielding his sex toys in ways that would make her hoarse from screaming by week's end.

"What's your name, sugar?" Dylan drawled from a few seats down.

The brunette released her lower lip from the vise of her teeth and said quietly into the microphone, "Jessie."

"Hooo, sounds like a cowgirl to me. You ever ride, Jessie?"

She shook her head.

"I'll have her straddling me in a few hours," Booker said from behind Jack.

Jessie flushed to the roots of her hair, but the corner of her mouth twitched as if she wanted to smile.

"Tell me, Jessie. Do you think of yourself as adventurous?" Dylan asked.

"Well, I travel a lot. I've hiked through the Redwood Forest and climbed Machu Picchu."

"Good...very good." Booker only had to drawl in his low voice and it sent a woman into a tizzy. Dylan might seem to be the cowboy in charge, but Booker was using his mysterious charm to lure her to him.

Jack sat back and watched.

"I don't think I'm going to let this opportunity pass," Jackson said from the end of the row. "I'm calling for her." With that, he pushed his button.

Dylan hit his next, and Booker was last. Their chairs were illuminated under brighter spotlights, giving Jessie a better view of her choices.

As she swung her gaze from one cowboy to the next, she shook with nerves. Jack hated seeing the girls so worked up, but it couldn't be helped. When they went home, they'd remember how nervous they'd been, and how everything had worked out so well.

Hopefully they'd carry that into their personal lives. Be empowered.

"Jessie, do you have an idea of who you might select?" Hugh asked.

Again, she looked from one face to the next. After a long minute, she nodded.

"Him." She raised a hand and pointed at Booker.

He released a cowboy whoop and jumped out of his chair. They all laughed as he jogged out of the row and toward Jessie. When he leaped the stage, Jessie took several steps back. But he didn't let her go far.

He scooped her off her feet in pure Booker style. She threw her head back, laughing, already looking more carefree than she'd probably felt in too long.

After that, they got rolling. In no time, six more girls stood trembling in the spotlight, and were swept away by the boisterous Boot Knockers. Every time another would walk onstage, Jack would release the breath he'd been holding.

Looking over Lissy's photo again, he tried to figure out what was so compelling about her. He'd had a lot of beautiful women in his time, and while she was gorgeous, it wasn't the reason he was drawn to her.

Stowe led another happy woman offstage. Jack fisted and unfisted his hand. Was she up next?

He stared at the black curtain, waiting for her to appear.

His heart skidded to a halt and restarted, double-time.

Lissy strode across the stage with a confidence they didn't often see here at the Boot Knockers Ranch. Self-assured.

And sexy as hell.

She wore a tank top and shorts, the edges of her sports bra peeking from beneath the straps of her top. Her hair was long and loose, warm brown waves with red highlights. And her breasts…

Jack's cock had jutted to its full eight inches at first sight.

He half stood from his chair, and someone pushed him down. He had to hear her voice. Heart pounding, he got right to business. He was known for his playful ways and a humor that won the girls over. Grinning, he prepared his first cheesy line. "I thought happiness started with an H."

A quizzical smile played about her full lips as she peered through the glare of spotlights at him. "It does."

"Then why does mine begin with U?"

Several guffaws and a smattering of applause, and Lissy smiled in earnest. Her skin glowed, lightly tanned from the outdoor sports she enjoyed, according to her file. Now that he'd gotten his goofy ice-breaker out, his mind fumbled over her information.

"What's your name, sweetheart?" someone drawled.

"Lissy Lofton."

Jack directed her attention back to him. "I see you spend a lot of time with horses, Lissy." God, her name felt good on his tongue. Was it his imagination or did her eyes hood?

He ached to stand and go to her, but as soon as he stood, she'd see the bulge in his jeans. He nudged his fly, trying to gain some breathing room, and a few cowboys laughed.

"I know my way around horses, yes. I've been a show jumper since I was ten. And I have a degree in equine science."

He liked her more with each syllable she spoke. From the corner of his eye, he glimpsed Paul, moving closer to the stage. Damn, he wasn't going to vie for her, was he? This was his week off.

"Tell us what you would wear swimming, Lissy," Ty said.

"Umm...a bikini?"

Jack launched to his feet and slapped his button before Ty could wheedle his way into this deal.

Lissy jerked, eyes wide. She absolutely fucking *glowed*. God, Jack couldn't wait to get her alone.

Paul wandered closer.

Ty hit his button, and then it was on.

Jack whirled toward him. "You'd better sit your inexperienced butt back in that chair."

Ty shook his head, extending a hand as if asking for Lissy to put hers in it. "I sense a connection between us, Lissy."

"Like hell," Jack grated out. Yeah, Ty was throwing her off by being so forward, pushing her right into Jack's arms, but the mere thought of him trying to schmooze her raised Jack's ire.

Eyes flashing, Ty continued. "My name is Ty, by the way. Choose me and you won't regret it, I promise."

A shadow of emotion sneaked through Jack's system. He wanted to call it anger, but that wasn't quite right.

He hit his button again, though it didn't light him up any more or convince Lissy to be his for the week. He just didn't know what else to do. All those lines he used to finesse flew out of his brain.

"Lissy..." he said simply, holding out a hand, palm up.

She zeroed in on him, cheeks tinged pink and her full lips tilted at the corners.

"C'mon, sweetheart," Ty said.

"Ty, I'm going to send you for new dentures," Jack practically growled, and everyone laughed, including Lissy.

Taking that as a good sign—she liked his humor—Jack pursued his cause. "I'm your cowboy, Lissy. Just say the word." He resisted the urge to say "please" because he'd never live it down.

But he was close to begging.

She glanced between him and Ty. Damn, the way she was looking at him made him feel all man.

Slowly, she nodded. "I pick Jack."

He fist-punched the air. Planting a hand beside the button, he vaulted over the long wooden desk and hurled himself forward to claim his girl. Someone hooted, and he ignored them, Lissy his only thought.

As he leaped onto the stage, she pivoted to face him. God, up close she was even more gorgeous. He reached for her hand, and without hesitation, she slipped hers into it.

Electricity shot up his arm to his shoulder and exploded through his whole body. She smelled like the rain, and her hair shone under the lights.

She only had to tip her head up slightly to meet his gaze. "Hi," she breathed.

"Hey, baby." His voice came out grittier than he'd meant for it to, but she didn't seem to mind.

He grasped her hand and looped it over his arm. She curled her fingers around the muscle of his forearm, sending new shocks of need to his throbbing cock.

"You made the right choice," he said.

Her eyes were dark blue and filled with something bright and wild, like the sea on a stormy night. "I never doubted."

* * * * *

How the hell had she known Jack's name? To Paul's recollection, Jack hadn't mentioned his name.

That meant she had learned it from Holly during the attraction selection process.

Damned if that didn't bother the fuck out of Paul. Why did this have to be his week off? He would have fought tooth and spur to win her.

Lissy.

Even her name was intriguing. Did it stand for Alyssa? Melissa?

He didn't stick around to watch the rest of the cowboys push buttons. He stalked back to the exit, trying to shake the image of Jack escorting Lissy offstage from his mind.

It had been a long time since he'd seen a woman who made him feel as nervous as a teenager again. Those long, long tan legs and the way she held herself — she was sexy as hell, and she knew who she was.

Most women who came to the Boot Knockers for help weren't so confident, and Lissy wore it like the most beautiful dress on the red carpet.

Visions toppled over one another in his mind. Easily he pictured her sitting on the bed, nude, totally comfortable in front of him.

Well, in front of Jack.

Damn the man. Why did Jack get all the luck?

The air was already heavy with humidity. They'd have a storm by nightfall, and that meant Lissy would curl up closer to Jack and ride out the storm, while Paul tossed and turned on his hard bunk.

His long strides devoured the distance between auditorium and barn. If rain was coming, he had some work to do. A downpour on sunbaked earth meant flooding, and there was one corner of the barn that was regularly engulfed in water.

No matter how many times he and Riggs had dug it up and placed a network of drain pipes underground, that corner was always wet. Sometimes the water would creep up the wall and drench the last two stalls inside. That meant wet horses.

As soon as he reached the barn, though, he veered right again, driven by pure instinct. He needed to get his hands on Lissy's file.

The office was empty because everyone was in the auditorium. Paul quietly closed the door and walked up to the wall of files. Holly was mega-organized. If he asked for a file, she could practically reach behind her without looking and pluck the folder from its spot. He hoped her L files were in order.

Laughlin, Larringer, Laverne. He skimmed through the alphabet to the LO section. Loahan. Lobrinsky. Lofton.

Heart pounding, he placed a fingertip on the top of the folder and eased it from its home. With the file in his hands, he spun to the desk and placed it on the surface, spread open.

This was the master file. The ones the Boot Knockers had back in the auditorium were a pared-down version. Paul's throat felt dry and sticky suddenly. He had more information about Lissy than Jack.

For now. Soon Jack would know more things about that striking woman than any other man on the planet.

She was a virgin — Jack's specialty. Not for the first time Paul wished he had a talent that set him apart. He'd never taken anyone's virginity, was crap with tying girls with rope, and he liked using his own cock rather than a rubbery plastic one.

Lissy was a West Coast girl who surfed, rode horses and recently had won a title in the semi-pro beach volleyball circuit. How had she gotten so far in life without getting laid? She had to possess other hang-ups that weren't evident on the typed page.

Quickly he shut the folder, and with it tucked tightly in his grasp, he left the office. Texas heat blasted him in the face after being in the air conditioning, and he sucked in a slow breath of what felt like water. He practically swam through the air to the bunkhouse, and by the time he reached it, his clothes were damp.

Hell, a man needed a cold iced tea after just walking between buildings.

He went to the mini-fridge where Teller hoarded bottles of soda and beer. The badass cowboy liked to threaten an ass-kicking to anyone who touched his loot, but Paul didn't give a damn.

He grabbed a bottle of cola and uncapped it. As he drank off half the contents, he ran his thumb over the file he held.

Precious information.

Why was he so fixated on Lissy and her life? He'd never done anything like this before. He obviously had too much time on his hands this week, and he hadn't gone very long without a client yet. By day six he was going to have a serious case of "the chafes" after jacking off to relieve himself.

As he softly belched around the bubbles he'd just swallowed, he moved to his bunk, his boots scuffing on the worn wood planks. He sank to his bunk and opened the file on his knees.

Lissy's picture was stunning. Where had she been when that was snapped? An outdoor party? A volleyball tournament? Strands of her warm brown hair were caught in an invisible breeze.

He leaned in and looked closer at the right corner of her mouth. Did she have a dimple? He hadn't remembered seeing it when she was onstage, but maybe she hadn't smiled wide enough.

He sipped the rest of the cola, feeling perspiration roll down his spine. What bungalow were Jack and Lissy in?

He flipped a few pages. Bungalow 15.

With a hollow stomach, he read Lissy's interview questions. Tell us your best memory. Where do you see yourself in a year? In five years? Damn, he didn't know the questions delved into a woman's mind so much. Holly processed this information in a way that benefitted the woman in the best possible way.

She was truly a master at what she did, and Paul admired her more after reading Lissy's file.

He was also growing more jealous of Jack with every word.

Planting one hand on the file so it didn't flutter to the floor, he rested back on his bunk, his arm slung over his eyes. The ceiling fans pushed the scantest bit of air his direction, but nothing would cool him at this point. He needed release — pure and simple.

He sat up and took care to close the file. Then he stashed it beneath his pillow. Lying down again, he flicked open his belt buckle with practiced ease. Anticipation ran through his veins as he unbuttoned his fly all the way. His cock lay semi-hard under his briefs.

Visions of Lissy and all the things he would do to her if she were his ran through his head. Tendrils of hair floating around him as she rode him. Lean thighs locked around his hips, and those dark blue eyes…

When his cock slid into his palm, it was hard and thick with want. Using one hand, he pressed his balls to his body while he slipped his erection through his palm. It wasn't often he was left to pleasure himself. Damn, since taking this job he'd become a real sex addict just like the rest of the Boot Knockers.

At one time he'd made fun of them for this very reason, but now he understood their suffering. When a man in his prime was accustomed to pleasure every day of his life, he found it difficult to go without.

A quiet groan escaped him as he pumped his cock. The head was fat and leaking already. The tension in his groin mounted as he ran his thumb under the cap. His hips bucked up, his buckle jangling.

How would Lissy taste? That lucky bastard friend of his was probably finding out right now. The Boot Knockers were fast movers with their clients. Their strategy of making a woman happy as fast as possible had always worked in their favor. Yes, they were sensitive to women who needed more time, but they also knew the ladies were here to be pushed out of their comfort zones.

His flesh heated against his palm. His cock lengthened another fraction. Scenarios played through his mind. Jack probably had Lissy stretched on the bed, her face glowing with bliss, her amazing hair spread around her, his fingers buried deep in her pussy.

Sweet scents of her arousal hanging around them, watching her pupils dilate as he reached that special spot on her inner wall. Pressing it, her juices flooding his fingers.

Those rough fingers Paul knew so well. Hell, he knew a lot about Jack. Like the scorching expression in his eyes just before he moved in for that kiss.

Spending too much time with Jack wasn't a good idea, especially drinking and hanging out on the ridge talking about women. Or the lack of women. Hell, Paul had almost welcomed the feel of Jack's lips on his.

The knot in Paul's stomach pulled tight. No, he did not want his best friend. No matter how close they'd become, he couldn't— wouldn't—think of Jack that way.

But as he tugged on his cock, the moments where Jack had taken advantage pushed into his thoughts.

His balls ached with the need for release. He moved his hand faster as the pressure became excruciating. He opened his eyes and stared at the revolving blades of the ceiling fan. But he wasn't really seeing—his sight was focused on the woman in Bungalow 15 with Jack.

He slid a finger between his balls in rhythm to the movements of his other hand. Would Jack have her delectable body trapped against a wall? Her breasts soft, her lips pliant beneath his?

When Jack breached her panties, would he find her bare or would he discover a small patch of curls? God, if only he could be the one to discover the wetness between her thighs.

The sound of his hand on his cock filled the air. His muscles stiffened, visions of Jack claiming her cries with one of his rough kisses while driving his fingers into her pussy searing Paul. Jack's beard stubble against her cheek—

In a blinding burst, he came. Spurts of hot cream covered his wrist and stomach as he pumped out his orgasm. A guttural grunt left him, and he held his breath through the final jets of his release.

When the last dribble strung between his swollen head and his body, he pushed out his breath. Heart throbbing in his temples, he tried to get his bearings, but all he could see inside his mind was Jack and Lissy.

He'd come for what had felt like a solid minute. When had he last unloaded this way? After only a day of abstinence, his body had rebounded with a lot of output.

He slowly sat up and grabbed a dirty T-shirt draped over his nightstand. He used it to wipe away the droplets. One clung to his finger, and he stuck it in his mouth. Salty-sweet. He'd heard that pineapple helped the flavor of semen, and he'd been partaking of a fruit smoothie every morning. Cook mixed up a big batch daily, and many of the cowboys swore by it. Paul had tried it as a result, and maybe it was working.

He zipped himself back inside his jeans, and leaving his belt undone, he flopped back on his bunk. Lissy's picture loomed in his mind, mingling with the slideshow of his imagination a few moments before.

Again, he envisioned her ripe breasts spilling from her tank top, Jack's lips moving over the straining nipples.

Paul moaned and threw himself to his feet. He had to get out of here. If he didn't, he'd spend half the day getting off to the porn playing in his head. No, he had to fix that wet area by the barn. The rain wasn't going to wait for him to slake his lust.

* * * * *

Lissy had come to the ranch to get in touch with her sensuous side. One look at Jack and she knew she'd made the right decision.

He was six feet of muscled, denim-clad hunk with a mischievous look in his eyes that spoke of his love for life. His hat was tipped oh, so low against the blazing sun as he led her away from the auditorium.

My Boot Knocker.

As they walked, his shoulder brushed hers, and their hips bumped. She resisted the urge to dig her fingers more solidly into his arm and yank him close. Suddenly the years she'd spent without a man seemed like a century. It was high time she had a man pressing her down on a mattress, his cock spearing her.

The light hairs on her arms raised, and he glanced at her. "Surely you're not cold. It's at least eighty-five degrees." The smile around his eyes suggested he knew she wasn't a bit cold — that she was reacting to his nearness.

Nerves made her voice crack. "Not cold." In fact, very hot. The tingle between her thighs was increasing.

Jack's hip bumped hers again, shooting need low through her belly. "So, Lissy." He drawled her name until her nipples puckered. "What do you do for fun?"

"Outdoor sports. Hiking. And of course, I ride."

He nodded, blue-green eyes twinkling. "I was hopin' you'd say that." He kicked up his pace, and she kept up, their legs nearly matched in length. She was glad to find he wasn't shorter than her. That had been one of her fears in choosing a man off the brochure. They all stood in a line, and it was impossible to tell how tall he was.

"Where are we going?"

"The barn. Just there." He pointed, and she smiled at the picturesque barn against the backdrop of sky. Puffy clouds dotted the blue, but they looked slightly bruised, as if they might release rain. "You were a show jumper."

"Yes." She relaxed as the scent of hay teased her nose. Musky, delicious man was too distracting.

"Tell me about that."

This felt far from an arranged date. As if she'd chosen him and he'd chosen her, and they were simply spending an enjoyable morning together.

Well, they sort of *had* selected each other. Out of twenty women, he'd wanted her.

Her heart quickened, and somehow she managed to find words to answer his request. "I've been riding forever, and it's always been my passion. When I got my first pony, I jumped him within a day."

"Wow."

She suppressed a shiver at his tone and the look in his eyes. She chuckled. "Well, it wasn't exactly intentional. The pony, Buttercup, was a little stroppy. She took off and I was inexperienced enough to not know how to put on the brakes. My mom was screaming her head off as she watched me take off across the field. But my dad" — she shook her head — "he had his hands on his hips and was smiling. That's how I knew I'd be okay."

The corner of Jack's mouth twitched upward. God, he was a beautiful man. Rugged, his jaw speckled with blond-brown hairs. His eyebrows were well shaped, but one had a crooked path through it—a scar where the hair didn't grow.

"He sounds like a smart man."

"How do you know that from two sentences about him?" She smiled into his eyes, and a warm kernel settled in her chest.

"He knew his daughter was capable of making the best of the situation she was in. You did, right?"

Feeling pride at his tone and confidence, she straightened to her full height. "Of course. Buttercup was out of control, heading right for the fence. I tried to use my heels to direct him to the open gate, but he was stubborn. So I held on, and when he got close enough to jump, I gave him a kick in the sides."

Jack pushed out a laugh. Heat licked her pussy, teasing in a way she'd never known.

"And then you were hooked on jumping."

"That sums it up, yes."

They were walking more slowly, and she realized he was trying to get to know her more before they reached the barn. Grass swished over her sandals. She glanced down to see her feet were nearly as big as Jack's.

Big feet, big…

She swallowed that thought before she turned to him and threw herself into his arms. Too easily she'd noticed the bulge in the front of his Wranglers. She ticked her gaze upward and found his zipper was still distended.

When she met his eyes, amusement creased his. Oh hell, he'd caught her looking.

"You like what you see?"

Was there any point in playing hard-to-get? She'd paid to be in his bed. "I do." She arched a brow in challenge.

But he caught her totally off guard.

"Me too, baby. I *really* like what I see."

Warmth rippled down her spine and settled on her buttocks. No, wait. That was Jack's hand.

Her breath caught as he lightly caressed the crest of her ass. A familiar longing captured her, and this time that need would be taken care of—and not by her own hand.

"Just this way." With that hand on her backside, he guided her around the side of the barn. Wildflowers grew as a border around the walls.

"It's a wonder the horses don't crop off all those flowers," she said.

"Naw. They don't like this kind, which is why they're still here. Notice there isn't a yellow flower in sight."

She laughed. It was so easy to laugh with him. Here she felt lighter than she'd felt in a very long time. Years of all-girls boarding schools and then college—decades of rules she'd followed to the last letter. Even volleyball was all rules. She hoped Jack didn't have any for her. For once she wanted free rein.

The inside of the barn was clean and brighter than she'd imagined. Her life had been a series of elite horse facilities with tile floors and a lot of windows. While this one was an old-fashioned wooden structure, several openings high on the walls sent shafts of light into the space.

She dragged in a breath.

Jack was watching her closely. "You like this life, don't you?"

"It's why I took up equine science." She moved away from Jack's side and wandered up to the first stall. An old paint mare stood dozing. She looked old but her coat was brushed, and she had fresh hay.

"That's Addie. She's been with Hugh forever. He actually brought her up from his family's ranch."

"Fifteen years old?" she asked, reaching for the horse's neck. She laid her hand on warm hide.

"Nineteen." Jack came to her side and leaned his elbows on the wooden door.

"She doesn't ride anymore, I'm sure."

"No, but Hugh takes her out for walks. The vet says it's what keeps her so healthy."

Lissy nodded in agreement. "Who is Hugh?"

"The master of games. You would have seen him standing in the auditorium, arms folded."

She flipped through her broken memories of the time she'd been onstage. A bundle of nerves, she'd barely registered anything besides the eyes on her. But now that she focused on the moments, she conjured the image of a huge cowboy standing beside the lines of cowboys. Actually, there had been two cowboys standing with arms folded.

With a jolt, she placed the other cowboy. The one named Paul, who Holly had suggested looked a little like that actor.

Yes, he did, and his gaze had been intense on her. Why hadn't he been seated with the others?

She patted Addie's neck. Jack leaned close, his scent washing over her. Her heart took off running faster than Buttercup had that long-ago spring day. Question was, could she guide it over the fence or take a better route through the gate?

It didn't matter. Jack was in control.

He snaked a hand around her nape, drawing her closer. Up close his eyes burned. He smelled so good. After years of women's body sprays and powdery deodorant smells, Lissy welcomed a man.

"It's good to know you react to me, Lissy." The way he drawled her name would forever be etched into her mind. This was exactly what she'd come here for—to have a man show her she was sexy and desirable. Women's pursuits didn't do it for her.

She looked at him sidelong. What did he expect of her? Was he waiting for a green light?

Ever so slowly he lowered his mouth to her skin. The first graze of his lips seared her. Having been touched so little, every nerve ending felt ultra-sensitive. She sucked in a breath and curled up like a pill bug when someone stroked it.

Jack's laugh was a rumble against her side. He took her shoulders and turned her to face him. His expression was genuine. Were his lips as firm as they looked?

"I don't think you're afraid of me."

"No," she said. "It's just that I've—"

"I know." He traced a path over her throat, over the place where her skin still burned from his kiss. If she lived to be a hundred, she'd always remember that first kiss from a man.

Gaze ensnaring hers, he zigzagged his finger down to her collarbone. Her breathing grew choppy as he snaked it back up and around to her cheekbone. When he brushed the callused tip over her lips, she issued a moan. She couldn't help it.

"Never been kissed, Lissy?"

She stared at his mouth hard. Her muscles were singing with awareness, her panties growing damp. She shook her head, and a wave of her hair fell over his wrist. Against his tanned skin, it fascinated her. But she could hardly keep from looking at him for long.

"Those lips were made for kissing," he drawled.

"H-how can you tell?" She was so ready. For years she'd ached for this moment, and now that it was here, she couldn't be happier with her choice of men. Even if he was a hired lover.

He smoothed his thumb back and forth over her lower lip, his stare awakening brand-new places in her body. Her breasts grew heavy and the nipples harder than ever.

"This lower lip is as ripe as a juicy peach. And this upper one"—he dragged his thumb over the rounded edges—"is a man's wet dream."

His dirty words spiked her desire. She wrapped her fingers around his strong wrist. Wide, sprinkled with light hairs, warm from the sun. Damn, she wanted to touch his every inch. For a week, Jack was hers to worship.

And she planned to take total advantage and make the big fee worth it.

His lashes lowered over smoldering eyes the color of sea glass. As a child she'd gathered the remnants from the beach and kept them in a little wooden box her parents had given her. What had happened to that collection?

Who cared? Now she had a new kind of sea glass to admire.

Jack tipped closer until the brim of his hat bumped her forehead. With a warm chuckle, he nudged it up. "Hat on or off, Lissy?"

Her mind bounced around the question. What did she want her first kiss to be like? He was allowing her to choose her path. Her heart swelled with the knowledge of her own power.

"On," she whispered, her voice a stranger's.

He angled his head, nose brushing hers. She filled her lungs with his scent—leather, man, hay. All the things she adored clinging to one perfect cowboy.

He nuzzled her, and she let her eyes slip shut. Jack's arms wove around her. She trembled in his hold, the feeling new and just right. His sculpted chest against hers, the way his biceps flexed.

"Baby?" he said so quietly she wouldn't have caught it if her senses weren't on high alert.

"Yes?" She opened her eyes to find his an inch away.

"It's on."

He kissed her.

His lips were warm and dry, softer than they appeared. Lissy's synapses fired—bottle rockets shooting into a warm summer night. She gasped, and the instant her lips parted, his tongue swept inside.

The first taste of Jack overwhelmed her. Passion struck her square in the chest, and she threw her arms around his shoulders. He groaned, the vibration sweet music. He locked her tighter to his body, molding her, as he deepened the kiss.

He slanted his tongue over hers, once, twice. When her knees threatened to buckle, he locked her to the stall door and held her up. She dug her fingers into his back as he stroked every inch of the inside of her mouth.

Decadent flavors overpowered her, and she gave herself up to this man. He sank his fingers into her hair and hauled her into the kiss. The everlasting, toe-curling, pussy-clenching kiss of a lifetime.

She grew bold enough to run her tongue around his, and he growled in response.

Dark tendrils of lust extended their fingers through her core. Her panties were a soggy mess, and her inner thigh muscles quivered.

Jack rocked his hips against hers.

She tore away from the kiss. "Oh God. Off!" She knocked his hat off his head, raising surprised rumbles of laughter that sang in her very soul.

She thrust her fingers into his soft hair and kissed him with all the pent-up need inside her. As if knowing this — hell, he probably knew more about women than most men on earth — he slammed his hips into hers.

The door shuddered, and some horses farther down shifted. One whickered softly.

Lissy drank in the moment — horse, man, deep kisses…and an erection bigger than the dildo in her nightstand drawer.

She pushed back against him, eager for more.

He lifted her, and she wrapped her legs around him. Their kiss grew more untamed as he carried her a few steps to a stall. When he kicked open the door, she laughed. He caught the sound with his kiss, his smile spreading over hers.

The hay was a soft cushion as he laid her down. His weight felt amazing, and his eyes were two deep pools. She fell into them headfirst.

He braced himself on his arms, his eyes clearing a bit. "This isn't the best place for your first time."

She looked at the knotted wood walls. Dust motes swirled around his head.

"Most women wouldn't want their first time to be in a horse stall, but I can't think of a better place."

His eyes hazed over again. "Really?"

"Yes," she whispered. Strands of his hair were silken under her fingers. She'd never imagined a cowboy would have such soft hair.

He issued a sound that made her nipples ache. "You're sure, baby?"

"Keep calling me baby and I'll do anything you want."

"This is about what you want."

She swallowed a lump of emotion in her throat and nodded. When she tangled her fingers into his hair further and drew him close enough to kiss, she found her words.

"Jack, this is better than any fantasy of an experienced woman with a vibrator."

He groaned and rocked his hips into hers. The hay shaped around her backside. She hooked her foot around his calf.

"You're telling me you've..." He stopped, expression intense.

She nodded. "Popped my cherry long ago. First on horseback coming down from a jump. Much later with a toy."

"Fuck," he breathed, dropping his forehead to hers. She was so glad to have gotten rid of his hat. "That means you can take me easily."

The ridge of his erection pressed into her belly. "Well, you're bigger than my toy, but yes, I think so."

This groan was more of a snarl. He plunged his tongue into her mouth, stoking her fires for long, dizzying minutes. A pulsation took up residence between her legs. Her clit was tight and hard, burning for his touch. Would he kiss her there? Stroke her hard bud with his tongue?

Jack withdrew from the kiss, watching her face as he worked a big hand up her torso to cup her breast. "Let me put down a blanket at least. Getting hay in certain body parts is no damn fun."

A giggle left her, and she nodded agreement. He pushed back to his feet and extended a hand. She let him pull her into a standing position, then he reached for a horse blanket draped over the wall.

As he flicked the cloth out, she stared at the muscles rippling under his tanned skin. In a few minutes, she'd have that warm flesh against hers — and his hard length plunging inside her.

She locked her knees to keep them from shaking and fisted her hands. When he had the blanket spread to his liking, he turned to her. She moved into his outstretched arms without hesitation, welcoming his now-familiar feel and scent.

He captured her lips once more, plying her into a boneless mass of girl-dreams. When he nibbled on her lower lip, though, the feisty woman took charge.

She sank her teeth lightly into his lower lip in return. His cock swelled against her belly, bigger and harder if such a thing were possible. He tugged her down to the blanket and covered her with his body. The first touch of hand to breast ignited her.

She couldn't hold still. She writhed and arched beneath his skilled hands. While he kneaded her breasts and plucked her nipples through her shirt and bra, she gazed up at him, committing every second of this coupling to memory.

He reached for her shirt hem, fingers grazing skin that had never been touched. She gasped. As he removed her top, then her bra, his eyes darkened. She quaked when he gazed at her breasts with a look of wild need.

The almost savage expression on his handsome face only spurred her on. She wrapped her legs around his waist as he dived for her breasts. He sucked one nipple into his mouth, pulling on it with a soft suction that made her come undone. Her pussy squeezed, juices pooling in her already soggy panties.

Masculine groans escaped him as he switched to her other nipple. She ran her fingers over his warm scalp as he stole her mind. He released her nipple with a *pop*. For some reason it made her giggle, but a heartbeat later she wasn't laughing anymore.

He kissed a path down, down her body, circling her navel at the same time he tugged down her athletic shorts. Was he expecting lacy thong panties? He probably saw many scraps of lace as a Boot Knocker, and her worry dulled her desire a little.

"White cotton panties. *Fuck*." He tore at them like a starving man ripping open a candy bar. She watched his face as he removed her sandals then pulled her shorts and panties off her body.

Jack shoved back to his knees and scrubbed both hands over his face.

Was that good or bad? Her heart thudded in her temples.

"Holy hell, baby. Your body... Christ, you're beautiful."

Heart beating triple-time, she reached for him. In seconds she'd stripped her first man. The removal of his T-shirt, the feel of sculpted muscle under her hands were the best moments of her life. Those nipple rings...

She shuddered.

When she unfastened his pants—and all five buttons of his fly—she stopped breathing.

His boxers were tented, the ridge of his cock revealing his desire.

In that instant, her number one reason for coming to the ranch was achieved. He wanted her.

She wet her lips, and he growled in response. He twisted and turned, kicking off boots, stripping socks off long, white feet. When his jeans and boxers lay in a wad on the hay, he leaned over her.

With her longing so close to being satisfied, she wrapped her arms around him, trying to bring his steely body on top of hers.

"Wait, baby. I need…" His breathing was irregular. "Condom."

She stared into his eyes as he slipped a condom free and opened the packet. "Can I…?"

His eyelid twitched. "You wanna?"

She had to lay hands on him. "Yes."

When she took hold of his erection and fitted the rolled rubber over the purple tip, his eyes rolled back in his head.

* * * * *

Shit, he was a goner. No way was he going to be able to last with this woman. His balls throbbed, and his cock oozed pre-come. If he didn't get hold of his needs right now, he'd never get through the next few minutes.

Her first time had to be perfect.

But knowing she'd fucked herself? That she wouldn't need downtime to keep from getting sore? Not all virgins were like Lissy. Jesus, he was going to blow.

He clenched his molars and tried to still his rapid heart rate as Lissy awkwardly rolled the condom over the head of his cock. She let go of the rolled edge, and it popped back off. She giggled, biting her lower lip.

He grinned at her and urged her to try again. This was her moment. He could endure a few more fumbling efforts.

He hoped.

As soon as she got the condom halfway down his shaft, he took over. With one precise move, he had it stretched to the base of his erection.

Lissy stared, her eyes wide and a few freckles standing out on her nose. Had she grown pale? Damn, he had to fire her up again.

Her nipples were heavy cherries jutting from full breasts. Not only was her belly flat, but lined with muscle. He'd never slept with a woman with a body like hers, and it turned him on like nothing else.

He pressed her onto her back again and spent long minutes kissing her. The touch of her tongue was less hesitant now, and he reveled in each velvety flip. When he kissed a path over her breasts, sucking each nipple in turn again, she began to move restlessly against him.

His blood pressure spiked as the scent of her need struck him — sweet, heady woman.

Running his tongue over his lower lip in anticipation of the treat he was about to feast upon, he looked into her eyes. This woman was ready to be plucked from the vine.

He dived between her thighs.

She cried out as his tongue met juicy flesh. Her folds were drenched, her clit as hard as a little pebble. He laved her outer lips, delighting in how she'd groomed herself. Bare underneath with a little triangle of brown curls.

He threaded his fingers through them and pinned her to the blanket.

Twisting under his licks, she moaned in time to the movements of her hips. His cock bobbed against his abs, ready for the final result. But first he had to get her off. Not only because she'd be relaxed and ready to take him but because he had to taste her orgasm.

He nibbled her inner thigh crease, down and across to her soaked opening. When he snaked his tongue into her body, she fisted his hair and ground against him.

Hell, this was as far from a virgin experience as he'd ever had. Lissy was bolder and knew what she wanted while some virgins were timid. She was a wildcat.

Wasn't that what Paul had called his last girl?

Jack curled his tongue in and out of her tight walls until she bucked. Knowing she was out of control, he ran the flat of his tongue up to her clit. A single revolution around the straining nubbin had her screaming.

He looked up the length of her body at her flushed face, her lips an O of ecstasy. He flicked her engorged clit back and forth until he felt the first pulsations of her pussy.

Driving a finger deep into her channel, he licked and fucked. Her eyes were open, glassy and fixed on him. When she sank her teeth into her bottom lip, he knew she was there.

She cried out. Contractions around his finger sent quivers up his arm. With a growl, he drew her orgasm from her, rounding her clit again and again while her fists thumped on his shoulders.

Withdrawing his finger almost to the tip, he held it there, his tongue still. She met his gaze, and the ghost of a smile kissed her full lips.

"Jack," she rasped.

He didn't need more of an invitation. He hovered over her, his cock full to bursting. *Hold on to it. Hold on.* His inward chant did nothing to soothe his rattled nerves, though. This woman was going to kill him.

He pressed his cock against her slick folds, and they shared a moan. He dropped his forehead to hers and stared into her fever-bright eyes. "I'm going to try to go slow —"

She hooked her foot around his ass and drove him into her pussy in one solid thrust.

Throwing his head back, he issued a possessed sound that made the horse in the neighboring stall rattle the wall. Squeaking gasps left Lissy, and Jack stared at her hard, trying to gather his wits.

Was she okay? Hurting?

"Dammit, I wanted to go slow."

"After so many years, I don't need slow," she said.

"Hell, yeah." He trapped her face in his hands and kissed her as he sank to the hilt. Her walls parted for him, accepting him, then nestled around his every aching inch.

His heart matched the tempo of his throbbing cock. Lissy shifted, rolling under him in a way that set him on fire.

He started to move. Slowly at first, holding her gaze. Moans, soft touches. Kisses that spiraled out of control. Then faster, grinding his body into hers as moans escaped her in intervals.

"Baby, I'm close. I can't—"

She swallowed his words on a kiss. The tender feel of her tongue, the soft cushion of her thighs…

He clamped off a roar, realizing she was coming. Her face reddened and she pulled Jack down.

With her bearing all his weight, he let go. Come shot up from what felt like his toes. His whole body shook with one of the biggest orgasms he'd had in his life. Lissy clamped around him, milking every inch as he spurted.

He'd trained himself to remain aware of his lover and not just drift off into the blissful after-haze. But that was hard to do with Lissy. His entire body felt like jelly.

She held him, and he tried to slow his breathing. When he gained a bit of control, he raised his head and looked at her.

Her eyes were shining, her face aglow.

"You okay, baby?" His voice sounded rough. As he noted the flutter of her pulse in her throat and the tears that swam in her eyes, a knot of some strong emotion gripped him. It was that same thing he'd felt when Ty had tried to lure her away from him during the selection.

He pressed his lips together.

She nodded, a smile melting her dazed expression into one of total happiness. The warmth of that smile wove through his system. "More than okay."

Staring into her eyes, he said, "Next time I'll have you in bed."

Her fingers convulsed on his spine, revealing how affected she was by him. If he didn't watch it, she'd make him into a cocky fool.

Leaning close, he pressed a tender kiss to her swollen lips. "Oh yes. I'll have you in bed, in the shower, on the table and against the wall."

Her eyes glittered with amusement. "That sounds a little tame after my first time just took place in a barn. What else have you got?"

Chapter Four

Sweat rolled down Paul's spine as he filled the water troughs. The big tank and a hose system they hauled around in the back of a pickup helped them get water to animals on all parts of the ranch.

He welcomed the physical labor. Working with his hands outdoors was quite different from using them on a woman in bed.

Gallons of water poured into the trough, and the animals gathered around him to drink. There were quite a few lactating cows, and they required a lot of water for milk production.

So far the herd was intact. Today the vet was coming to check out the hurt calf and would most likely release it to pasture.

The faraway whine of an engine drifted to him. He glanced over his shoulder at the ranch below. The valley was still, not a cowboy in sight. No Jack, no Lissy. Not that Paul could make out their figures from this distance.

Well, maybe Jack's. The man had pressed himself against Paul enough times that he knew him more intimately than he'd like. That kiss the other night hadn't been the first and probably wouldn't be the last.

Each time Jack laid one on him, Paul grew less shocked by it. Someday he'd convince Jack to stop, or maybe Jack would convince him to stop fighting.

Paul swiped a hand over his face. He didn't want more than friendship, no matter how strange the flutters in his stomach when Jack pushed himself on him. He didn't know what his talent was in bed, but he knew what it *wasn't*.

He didn't know how to touch a man. Or be touched by one.

That wasn't entirely true either. Each time Jack laid his hands on Paul, he relaxed his guard a little more.

He threw himself into his work for another long hour while these thoughts circled his mind. Since becoming a Boot Knocker, he'd learned more about himself daily. Could he be learning to open his mind to being with men?

Even as the idea took hold, he stomped on it. He could no sooner picture himself with Elliot than riding in a limousine and living in a penthouse. But Jack might be different in bed.

Not because he was into Jack, of course. Only because he and Jack were so close.

With a huffing sigh, he finished his task and stared across the field again.

Jack was holed up with his sexy vixen, which was where Paul wanted to be.

Paul had rubbed off another lung-burning orgasm to thoughts of her. Of them. He should feel guilty for removing her file from the office and thinking of her this way when she wasn't his.

He slung the hose over his shoulder and headed back to the truck. He coiled the piping in the bed and checked the amount of water remaining in the tank. Good thing it had rained—they had plenty of water at least.

Leaning against the side of the old truck, he slipped off his work gloves and stared down at Bungalow 15.

Too easily he imagined Jack and Lissy in bed, limbs entangled, lips moving in a slow morning kiss. Jack certainly never wasted time deflowering a virgin, and the way he'd looked at Lissy was testament to his attraction to her.

How would Paul have handled her? He would have plied her with food and a little wine to loosen her up. Follow that with some candles and a massage.

Jack would have done things very differently, though.

Paul needed to know how the event had gone down. What had Jack done, said?

He pondered ways to get this information from his friend. In the distance, some dark birds took flight, circling above the trees.

"Shit," he said, pulling away from the truck. In two strides he reached the driver's door, yanked it open and slid into the old vinyl seat. He twisted the key in the ignition and bounced down the dusty trail leading to the patch of trees on the slope of the opposite hill.

Buzzards meant trouble—dead livestock.

While he and Jack had time invested in beef, Hugh and Riggs ran an elite horse herd. Just below that hill, their horses roamed. At night Riggs drove them into a corral, but a foal might have escaped his notice and become prey.

When Paul reached the hollow, he stopped on this side of the narrow creek that was dry except after a rain. He continued on foot. He sloshed through the shallow water to the bank, his heels cutting into the muddy grass.

The buzzards continued to wheel overhead, some swooping lower with each pass.

Squinting at the hillside, he tried to spot the reason the birds were here. As he angled up the hill, he saw it—a small brown hump.

"Shit." Too small for a foal, which was good. Too late in the summer for a fawn. But it might be one of the goats. The ornery buggers were forever breaking free and wandering the ranch.

When he neared, the wind ruffled feathers.

Ah—he stopped. One of the free-range chickens that supplied the ranch with eggs.

With a sigh, he strode to the dead animal. He crouched before it, inspecting it. Its neck was broken. Something had bitten it in the neck.

He caught the feet in one hand and hefted it. Carrying it back to the truck, he threw it in the back. They tried to keep the ranch free of sights like dead chickens to keep from disturbing the clients. Once they all started to emerge from the bungalows, they'd walk and ride, and they couldn't happen upon dead livestock.

Paul got back in the truck and drove toward the main buildings. After parking and opening the water tank to allow more rainwater to be collected, he went far off into the tree line and dug a hole for the chicken.

No one disturbed him. In fact, no one was around. Even Holly, Isabel, Hugh, Riggs and Sybill were hidden from view.

He covered the dead chicken with dirt but stole looks at the ranch, wondering what Jack and Lissy were doing.

He backhanded the sweat off his forehead and replaced his shovel in the barn. Then he went to the outdoor old-fashioned water pump. He washed his hands and scrubbed the sweat from his face and neck.

Still no one emerged from Bungalow 15.

"Son of a bitch," he murmured.

Maybe he'd check out the grub house, see if anyone was there.

What was his problem? Before he'd become an official Boot Knocker, he'd spent all of his days alone, working around the ranch. He'd had occasional help, but he was a loner.

Well, he used to be. When had he become such a social creature?

The sound of a door opening was like a shot to his system. He jerked, and shielding his eyes from the sun, he stared at Bungalow 15, hoping for a glimpse of the inhabitants.

A broad cowboy emerged from the neighboring bungalow. He was hatless, his shaggy brown hair mussed. He stood on the small porch and stretched his arms overhead, twisting right and left. Then he wandered down the steps and across the yard to the grub house.

Well, Paul would have Ty for company for breakfast at least.

The decadent scents of honey buns filled the space. Paul's stomach rumbled, and he went directly to the sideboard. Ty was already filling a plate with buns and fresh fruit.

"How's it going?" Paul asked.

Ty gave a craggy smile. "Tired as hell. She kept me up all night."

Paul snorted. "And that's different how?"

Ty leaned close. "She wanted anal."

Straightening, Paul stared at him. "On the first night?"

Nodding, Ty added a few slices of melon to the plate. A satisfied smirk twisted his lips.

Sure, Paul had experienced the pleasure of entering a forbidden spot, but not often. And certainly never on the first night. Usually it took a few days for the girls to reveal their kinks.

"She says her last boyfriend thought it was dirty. He wouldn't do it. And the guy before him too."

Paul shook his head. "Too many guys have hang-ups that give women complexes."

"And men too."

Paul rocked back a little on his heels. While Ty fixed himself a cup of coffee, Paul studied his words. Was he one of those men? He'd grown up in a family that had strictly opposed any same-sex relations. He'd absorbed their beliefs without giving any thought to his own.

He wasn't opposed to it anymore—if the guys consented and enjoyed it, who was Paul to judge?

Paul wished Jack was here to discuss these ideas.

"We have too many people in our lives who interject their opinions," Ty said, cradling his mug.

"Sometimes it's hard to shut up." Paul was surprised to hear his own words.

"Well, you've a right to speak your mind."

"Not if it stirs a hornet's nest. You know what they say about opinions. They're like assholes—everyone has them." Paul wasn't proud of telling off Riggs about sleeping with men. He'd never do that now. Shame burned his cheeks, and he dipped his head to hide it from Ty. After his last blow-up with Riggs, he'd confided in Jack that he felt bad about the whole affair, especially knowing Riggs was just following his heart.

He'd also confided to Jack that he'd found himself aroused when stumbling upon Riggs and Hugh hidden behind the barn one day. Jack had only nodded silently, but Paul chalked up the heat he'd felt in his groin to having a dry spell in his sex life.

After Jack had kissed him on the ridge, he'd thought about the leap of desire he'd felt when seeing Riggs and Hugh. Mainly because he'd felt that leap again.

He pressed his lips together.

"Amen, brother." Ty set a plate on a tray and added two bottles of milk. Shooting Paul a glance and a smile, he said, "I corrected her misconception that what she wanted was bad."

What about Lissy? Had Jack helped her through some emotional glitch too?

That bothered the hell out of Paul. He ran his knuckles over his upper lip, his facial hair prickling. Many of the Boot Knockers neglected to shave as often as they should because it seemed the women preferred the ruggedness. They came to Texas for an experience, and that included old-fashioned beard burns.

Jack's beard prickled but was also a little soft—

Wait. What the hell was he thinking?

Ty swung away from the buffet. "Well, I'd better get back to Marianne. She needs sustenance after screaming my name half the night."

Despite his inner discomposure, Paul laughed. "Enjoy."

Pausing, Ty asked, "What are you doing with your week off?"

Suffering.

He waved a hand in the direction of the cows he'd just watered. "Tending the herd."

"It's a good week to have off, seein's how they just arrived. You're clear to take care of any problems."

"That's probably why Holly assigned me off. She knows more about us than we do. Hey, have you heard anything about dead chickens?"

Ty bobbed his head. "Riggs mentioned it yesterday on the way to the auditorium. He thought it was a fox. You might want to try trapping it."

"Yeah, I thought of that. If it's killing our animals, it isn't welcome on the ranch."

The door opened and he looked up, heart lurching.

His face tingled from the momentary adrenaline rush, but it wasn't Jack or Lissy. Hugh wandered in with a grunt. He beelined for the coffee and poured a mug without looking at either of them.

"I'm off. Have a good one, Paul."

"Yeah, you too."

As Ty left, Paul watched him. Lucky bastard.

"You finding things to do on your week off?" Hugh asked, surprising Paul. He rarely spoke so early.

"Yeah, been up since dawn and in the field already."

Leaning against a nearby table, Hugh sipped his coffee. "That's good. If you run out of things to do, Riggs could use a hand."

"Yeah?" He and Riggs's history of animosity gave Paul a guilty feeling.

Hugh took a drink of steaming coffee. A second later, he said, "We've had some trouble with an A/C unit."

"Where?" *Please let it be in Bungalow 15.*

"In our house."

"I'll go on up and see if I can help Riggs."

"I'd appreciate it." Hugh went back to his coffee.

Paul selected some sausage and pancakes, needing a hearty breakfast if he was doing hard work. He shoveled it into his mouth and left the grub house after Hugh.

Without the guys to joke with or a lady to cater to, he felt a little lost. Glancing at his watch, he found it was the top of the hour. The vet should be driving up that dirt road right now, dust flying behind his truck.

Paul kicked around the barn, checked on horses. He hefted bags of feed from here to there. All the while he kept an eye on Bungalow 15. He was dying to get a glimpse of Lissy. Would she look rumpled and satisfied, as Paul had imagined her during his solo sessions?

Damn, he was losing his mind. At one time he'd loved the quiet work that sustained him and kept the ranch beautiful and running smoothly. Now he couldn't wait to get into bed with someone.

A step behind him made him swing around. But he knew who it was before he even met the pair of blue eyes. He'd known Jack a long time, and even the way he walked had become familiar.

"Hey." Jack offered a crooked smile and doffed his hat to scrub his fingers through his mussed hair.

"Hey." Paul's voice sounded brittle, probably because his heart was doing some odd flipping thing in his chest.

"I wanted to see if the vet had been here yet."

"Nope."

"When do you expect him?" Jack drifted closer, still holding his hat.

Scuffing his boot on the barn floor, Paul said, "He hasn't called. I expect soon."

"Everything else going okay?" Jack was in his space again, but that was nothing new.

Paul nodded. "It's been awfully quiet." Jack had found his way into Paul's space again, but that was nothing new.

Jack's grin widened. "You're used to hearing moans and screams all day and night, man."

Paul settled his gaze on Jack's. "And I'm used to talking to you."

Jack tipped his head, eyes hooding. As Jack leaned in to press his lips to Paul's, he anticipated his move. Paul could have shoved him away, but he waited, heart pounding. That need he'd felt last time—and when he'd run across Riggs and Hugh—was it really about something more?

When Jack's warm, dry lips met his, he closed his eyes instinctively.

Jack jerked.

Paul's eyes flew open.

"Paul..."

"What are you doing here anyway? You should be taking care of your woman. I can handle the animals."

Jack clamped his fingers around Paul's forearm, eyes too close, too bright. Paul could still feel Jack's prickly-soft beard against his own jaw. He twisted his arm from Jack's grasp.

"Go on back to Bungalow 15. I've got it covered."

"What was that, man? You closed your eyes."

"Tryin' to tolerate your ass." Paul's attempt at a joke fell flat. He sighed. "Just go on."

"All right."

After Jack's steps faded, Paul rubbed his face with his hands and tried to make sense of what had just happened—what he'd let Jack *do*. He'd let him kiss him. Hell, he'd almost invited it. Paul liked having Jack's attention, which might have been why it annoyed him so much to see Jack hitting on Elliot. And Riggs and Hugh had been friends for a long time before their relationship shift. Damn, his thoughts were tangled. He didn't know what to think.

He looked up to see the familiar cloud of dust traveling up the drive to the ranch—the vet come at last. Paul pulled on his work gloves. He had work to do, and there was no time to reflect on Jack or why Paul had allowed him so close. Or closed his eyes when Jack had kissed him.

Paul watched the vet climb out of his vehicle. Shoving away thoughts of Jack, Paul walked out to meet the vet, smiling.

He was as crusty as they came. Known for his bluntness as well as his old-fashioned philosophy when it came to animals, he was a perfect choice for the Boot Knockers.

"Ennis, how are ya?" Paul stuck out his hand and met the man halfway to the barn.

The man had thick white hair that often stuck up in wild directions, as he couldn't be bothered with a hat. His work dungarees were usually dirt-spattered — or worse. But he always arrived with a smile and sound advice.

"Good to see you, Paul. How's the calf?"

"Doing well. We're just waiting for your word to return her to the field."

He nodded and slapped his gloved hands together. "Let's take a look."

All business, he strode to the barn. Ennis examined the calf, lifting each leg and inspecting hooves, ears, eyes. When he was finished, he gave a satisfied grunt. "Get it back to the field. It's not favoring the leg. You've been feeding it grains, so it should be okay with being weaned early."

Paul nodded. "Sounds great. Thanks for coming."

"Any more critters for me to look at today?"

"I don't think so. But I'm sure I'll be in touch again."

They shook hands again and Paul saw Ennis back to his truck. Then Paul got his horse and saddled it. When he lifted the calf onto the saddle, the horse didn't budge. Paul swung up behind the calf, and clutching it with one hand and the reins in the other, he took off for the ridge.

As he crossed the field, he couldn't resist glancing back at Bungalow 15. He rubbed his jaw where Jack's beard had grazed his skin.

* * * * *

Lissy lay in a cocoon of warm bliss in Jack's arms. Her nose rested against his biceps, his spice growing more familiar to her with each breath she took. He'd gone out for a few minutes then crawled back into bed with her, skin cool and smelling of grass. She nuzzled it.

After keeping her awake all night, no wonder he was sleeping now. She was feeling the effects of too little sleep as well, but she was too wired to close her eyes.

Her first experiences had been more than she'd ever hoped for. Sweet, fun, sexy and tender. Jack was a playful lover, which was exactly what she'd needed. And God, was he thorough.

Her pussy still tingled from hours of licking, fingering and fucking. He'd given her how many orgasms? Eight? She'd lost count. Two in the barn, one before they'd barely gotten in the door of the bungalow. He'd pinned her to the wall and claimed her mouth while blowing her mind with his nimble fingers.

Then there was the bed in several positions.

"I see you're a morning person." Jack's low voice broke through her fog.

She shifted her gaze to his and smiled. He looked tanned and dangerous with that five o'clock shadow and his unsmiling mouth, sexy as hell against the stark white sheets. When his mouth quirked up, his smile extended to his eyes.

"I couldn't fall asleep."

"Oh, baby. Are you uncomfortable?" He leaned onto one elbow to stare down at her. For some reason, after all the intimacies they'd shared, this felt more personal. A warm knot formed in her belly.

"Not a bit uncomfortable. I think I was just too keyed up to sleep. I get that way sometimes before competitions."

"Hmm." He pressed a kiss to her bare shoulder, raising an immediate shiver from her.

She snuggled closer, listening to his breathing. Was it normal to feel so close to your first lover? She'd heard her friends discuss how they had "fallen in love" with their firsts, but this was completely different.

Lissy was no young girl, and she'd ended up with Jack in a very unconventional way.

Still, she couldn't bring herself to feel a hint of guilt for it. Especially when his arm lay warm and heavy across her middle, anchoring her to his side. During the long night she'd reveled in the crisp hair on his chest and legs, the hard ridges of muscled abs and that dark look in his eyes.

Did he look at all the girls that way?

She roused. "I'm going to brush my teeth and shower."

"Mmm." Apparently he wasn't much of a morning talker. When she tried to move, he threw his thigh over hers. His soft cock against her hip began to swell.

Her nipples puckered, and he clamped his fingers around one. The light pressure was enough. She went from zero to lust in seconds.

"Don't get up yet." His eyes smoldered as he gripped her hips. A mischievous tilt of his lips and she was flipped on top of him, straddling him.

Her folds were still wet from her orgasmic high and he groaned. Seated atop him should feel awkward. Shouldn't she feel shy or embarrassed? Her nipples jutted at him like two headlights, and her pussy was so…wet.

Testing her power, she rubbed against him and was rewarded with a total-body shudder. "Damn, baby, you're so ready."

She stared down at him. If any other cowboy was under her, would she be so turned on? Would her heart be racing so much?

Jack cupped her breasts, and she leaned into his touch. When he thumbed her nipples, an invisible string between his skin and her pussy stretched tight.

Need gripped her. She rocked against him, gliding his swollen head against her folds. His jaw did that leaping-muscle thing in the crease. More than once she'd noted it, and usually when he was taking deep, controlled breaths.

She hadn't explored him much, but it was time. She leaned forward and kissed his neck. The salty flavor of man spurred her on. She spattered kisses across his chest and dragged her teeth over one supple nipple. The small gold hoop under her tongue was warm.

He moaned, clasping her head in one big hand. She flicked her tongue around the bud, watching his satisfaction ripple across his handsome face. Trying to hide her grin and failing miserably, she suctioned her mouth over his other nipple while grinding against his full erection.

He was hard and long and thick, everything she'd never believed she'd have. Jack's eyes darkened, and she grew bolder. Nipping a path down his amazing abs, she memorized the feel of him. Each contour made her juices flow a little more.

He snaked his fingers through her loose hair and guided her. His cock was magnificent. It pointed upward, the tip red and glistening. A bead of pre-come was collected in the depression, begging her to taste it.

She'd never—

She parted her lips around his arousal.

"Jesus hell," he growled, hips lifting off the bed.

She swallowed another inch of his cock, aware of the fullness in her mouth and how it had felt in her pussy just hours ago. She wriggled restlessly against the mattress. His muscled thighs strained as he bucked upward.

"That's it, baby. Ever sucked a cock before?" His eyes were a stormy sea.

She shook her head, his shaft still in her mouth. It slipped in another inch, and Jack gnashed his teeth.

"Take me," he said after a long, panting minute. She was ready when he pushed to the back of her throat. A low moan escaped her. She'd never really seen the allure of sucking cock, but now she knew how wrong she'd been. Having him in her mouth was almost as good as her pussy. Besides, the way his mouth had tormented her, she wanted to return the favor.

Testing herself — and him — she ran her tongue down the side.

"Ahhh." His strangled cry said she'd done it just right. She tried the other side, swirling her tongue around his cap. Again, he pressed on her nape, commanding her.

Her pussy flooded. Sucking him from root to tip, she watched what her loving could do to him. His eyes rolled up in his head, and every muscle from jaw to groin strained. She guessed his toes would be curled too, if she could see them.

Splaying her fingers over his inner thighs, she yanked another growl from him. She blinked. He must be sensitive there, as she was.

She lightly caressed his thighs then balls. Another drop of pre-come struck her tongue, and she moaned. How would it feel to take his essence into her mouth?

What if she kissed him after he released?

Dark need drove her on. She licked down his cock to his balls. He almost came off the bed. She laved his tight sac and wiggled her tongue underneath.

"Ffffuck. Lissy, baby, do you know what you do to me?"

She could see it. She wanted him to lose control as she had with him.

Wildly, she sucked the head back into her mouth. With pressure on his shaft and her tongue dancing along the veined length, she explored the smooth skin under his balls with her fingers.

Jack's shaft lengthened another inch. "Baby, it's close. Keep doing that and I'll lose it."

"Mmm." She traced a circle in that spot with a fingertip. Again. And again.

He breathed fast and hard. In a rush, he came. Hot juices filled her mouth and she swallowed. The heated drops tasted sweet and salty at the same time — all Jack. She pressed her tongue against the spurting head, gathering every drop.

As his cock twitched between her lips, she ran a hand down his thigh. The final traces of his passion spent, he issued a ragged breath. Mouthing him gently, she watched his face.

He was a damn beautiful man with the stamina she needed this week. She hoped he could keep up with her, because she was just feeling the first awakenings of her true self.

When she let him slide from her mouth, she moved up his body to kiss him. She stroked his tongue with hers, and he growled. With a hand clamped to the back of her head, he devoured her. Tongue thrusting in and out until she burned.

Jack tore from the kiss and flipped her into the mattress. She bounced twice, and he caught her before she tumbled off the side of the bed. Laughing, he locked his palms on her thighs and spread her legs.

Her pussy lips felt slightly sore, but she wanted him so bad.

"Think you can get away with such behavior first thing in the morning, woman? It's time for your punishment."

With that, he delved between her thighs, tongue extended.

Joy burst in her chest as she succumbed to his sweet torture. Her last thought was that her money had been well-spent.

* * * * *

Their shared shower had been one of the more feisty ones Jack had ever had. She'd squirted half a bottle of shampoo on him and set about lathering him until his skin was white.

Of course, he'd returned the favor, concentrating on her pussy and breasts. He'd had no intention of fucking her again so soon, but the small squeaks she emitted had thrown him off the edge.

After taking her hard against the shower wall, and a mutual screamed orgasm, she'd gone boneless. Sweeping her into his arms, he'd said, "It only took nine orgasms to tire you out."

She giggled, soft and pliant and damp against his chest. "Ten."

He stared into her eyes. Small sapphire flecks circled the center, shining with amusement. "Really? Ten?"

"Uh-huh. I guess you lost count."

"Guess I did." He put her on her feet and wrapped her in a towel. She sagged against him, and he took his time drying her with the plush terrycloth. Wet tendrils of hair covered her shoulders, and he got another towel for it.

"Come with me. I'll dry your hair." He took her hand and led her into the bedroom, where he seated her on the bed. With her cross-legged and facing him, he set about toweling her hair.

As he worked the water from each strand, she stared at him. Trying like hell not to notice the way the towel she wrapped around her torso cracked open at her hips to reveal a long sliver of tanned inner thigh.

"You're still wet," she said quietly.

"I don't mind air-drying." His gaze flashed to hers. The intimate rope that had tethered them together for the past twenty-odd hours pulled tighter. Suddenly Jack couldn't remember the last woman he'd been with.

How terrible that he couldn't recall her name or the color of her eyes.

Swallowing hard, he continued to rub Lissy's hair. She leaned into his touch like an affectionate kitten. That new emotion emerged in his chest again—warm and prickly at once. What the hell was it? Pretty soon he'd have to figure out what it meant before he was forced to start charging it rent.

When she gripped his hips, his body reacted. A single touch and he was hard and aching again.

She licked her lips. "You haven't had ten orgasms yet."

"No, but I intend to. Just not all at once." He grinned at her enthusiasm. She was the best virgin he'd ever bedded.

"Your body says it's time." She curled her fingers around his hips, digging lightly into his ass.

Tilting his head, he gave her a crooked smile. "That's all your fault, baby."

God, her eyes actually darkened as he drawled the words. Her reaction was so damn perfect, it was a battle to keep from pushing her back on the bed.

But no.

"I wouldn't be a very good lover if I let you starve. Aren't you hungry? We missed dinner last night."

She nuzzled his hand as he cupped her face. "I never gave a thought to food."

"I know, but it's time to feed you. Maybe a nap first?" Her eyelids were heavy and she was blinking more and more slowly.

She rested her chin in his hand. "Maybe a short one."

"Good. Lie back here." He helped her into a comfortable position and covered her with a sheet. When he leaned over to kiss her between her long, perfect brows, she squeezed her eyes shut.

He lingered over her fruity scent and withdrew. Her eyes were hazy with fatigue.

"Sleep a bit, and then we'll go to the grub house for the best brunch you've ever had. Cook goes all out, and you won't want to miss it."

Her smile was wide and sweet. "Sounds good. Are you coming to bed?"

Staring down at her, it was easy to lose his bearings and forget who he was and why she was here. He had a hankering to crawl in bed with her and never surface.

Shaking himself, he smiled back at her. "You sleep. I have a few duties around the ranch to see to."

"Like what?"

God, he loved the way she brushed his knuckles with her silken fingers. "A new herd of beef and a hurt calf. If you sleep and eat, I promise to take you to see them later."

"That sounds good." Her voice trailed off, and he pressed another kiss between her brows.

"Sleep, baby. I'll be back for you."

He threw on his jeans from yesterday and bundled his shirt, boxers and socks under his arm. Then, carrying his boots in one hand, he crept from the bungalow. Coming out of the cooler space into the baking heat, he squinted at his surroundings.

"He can walk. I bet she can't," a familiar voice drawled.

He descended the few stairs to the turf, curling his bare toes into the grass. Paul stood leaning casually against the porch railing, one thumb hitched in his jeans and looking sexy as hell.

The hard-on he'd refused to let Lissy satisfy swelled for his best friend. Grinning, Paul pulled away from the railing. He and Jack fell into step, comrades as always.

"Everything okay with the herd?" Jack asked.

"Yeah, why?" He shot Jack a look, ice-blue eyes so different from Lissy's yet affecting Jack no less.

"I just thought…you searching me out…"

"Ennis cleared the calf to return to pasture, so I took it up. I thought you'd want to know."

Jack nodded. "Sounds good. I'm heading to get changed."

"I'll come along. I need to check on something."

They strolled toward the bunkhouse. Since most Boot Knockers were out with their ladies in the bungalows or around the ranch, no one was inside. Two bunks separated Jack's from Paul's. Countless times he'd wished he could push his up beside Paul's, but of course his friend wouldn't welcome such an advance.

After having Lissy's soft body tormenting his all night, Jack was shocked by how much Paul's hard form turned him on.

Paul strode to his bunk and tossed his hat on it. Then with his back to Jack, he lifted the edge of his pillow and peeked under it.

"You hiding a girl under there for your week off?" Jack joked.

Paul threw a look over his shoulder. Was that worry Jack detected on his face? "If I were, she'd be awfully skinny. You know I like a little meat on my girls."

Actually, Jack hadn't discovered a pattern in Paul's preferences. Holly and the clients selected the Boot Knockers, but in the end, sometimes lust won out and the guys would go crazy pushing buttons. But Jack couldn't remember anyone who had spun Paul's head.

Jack dropped his dirty clothes into a pile beside his bed and placed his boots on the floor. Facing his friend from across a few bunks, he unzipped his jeans. His cock was full and ready when it popped free.

Paul looked away.

Pushing his jeans off, Jack spun to rummage in the few drawers that held every piece of clothing he owned. He didn't need much more than a few pairs of jeans and some Boot Knockers T-shirts, especially when he spent most of his days in the buff.

He located a clean pair of boxers and some jeans and laid them on his bunk. When he looked up, Paul was staring at him.

Jack's heart clenched, but he quickly dismissed Paul's attention. He wasn't interested in men. How many times had he reminded Jack of this?

Fighting his arousal, Jack stepped into his boxers. "I'm not sure what your type is, Paul. Care to enlighten me?"

Paul grunted.

Jack looked up at him. "Tall or short?"

"Tall," he said at once.

"Yeah? Lately I've been into tall girls too. There's a lot to be said for not bending in half to kiss them."

Paul gave a short laugh and watched as Jack pulled on his jeans. Without bothering to zip and button them, Jack sat on the edge of his bunk facing Paul. "So you like a little cushion for the pushin', eh?"

Paul's teeth were very white against his tanned skin. "Beauty comes in all sizes."

"Absolutely true." Jack found a clean pair of socks wadded on the floor beside his bed and hitched his ankle over his leg to put one on. Again, Paul's stare conjured images of luring him to Jack's bunk, of pressing him down and sinking into his hot, tight ass.

His cock bulged at the waistband of his boxers, and Jack leaned back to adjust it.

Shaking his head, Paul laughed. "You're always raring to go, aren't you?"

"Can't help it. Besides, I turned down the virgin just a little bit ago. She needs some recovery time. She thinks she's ready for more, but she needs a break. I've done this enough to know."

Paul's face grew serious. "Lissy?"

"Yeah."

"Man, she must have been really ready for this vacation if she's asking for more."

"She was ripe, that's for sure. No shy virgin, and no pain because she's had penetration before."

"But—"

"Toys." Jack smiled.

"Damn, now I'm getting a chub." Paul nudged his fly to make room for the fat bulge there. Jack's eyes hooded. If only his friend would lie back and let Jack suck him off...

Lips pressed together, he tugged on his other sock and put on his boots. "Anyway, do I need to do anything for the herd? I left Lissy sleeping and thought I'd do a spot of work before I return to the bungalow."

Paul's Adam's apple bobbed in his throat. He raked his fingers through his light hair. "Not for the herd, no. They're watered. The calf is fine, and I checked on the others. I'm going to lend Riggs a hand later with his air conditioner."

"We can't have Sybill melting."

They exchanged a grin. Riggs and Hugh worshipped the woman who had arrived at the ranch with a case of sexual dysfunction. They'd quickly lightened her burden and refused to let her leave.

Paul swung his legs up and stretched out on his bunk. He eased a hand under his pillow, and his face froze at the swishing noise.

Curiosity piqued, Jack tried to think of what Paul was hiding. "Whatcha got there? Paper dolls?" He jerked his chin toward Paul's pillow.

"Nah, I could use a blow-up doll, though. Who knew I'd be so horny after one day off?"

Jack stood and took a step closer. He could leap the two bunks between them and pin Paul to the bed in the time it took a cowboy to wink. His cock distended another fraction, and he didn't bother to adjust it, allowing Paul to witness his full arousal.

For him.

For Lissy.

Damn, now he was seriously throbbing.

"You need some relief," Jack said slowly, hoping he got the hint.

"I've had a few solo sessions."

Dark waters of need gushed over Jack, and he drowned in images of Paul pumping his cock, spurting over his fingers.

"I'd be happy to help," Jack said before he thought better of it.

Paul went dead still, as he always did when Jack made an advance. "We've been over this already." But his eyes flashed and he ran his tongue over his lower lip.

Uncomfortable gesture or desire?

Paul got off the bunk and drifted closer. Jack tensed. Damn, what was going on?

"I hear I'm pretty good in bed," Jack said.

Paul forced a laugh. But he inched closer.

Jack folded his fingers into fists, fighting the need to grab his best friend and kiss the hell outta him. He'd wanted this for so long, but the cues Paul was giving pointed to him softening toward Jack. He couldn't risk scaring him off by being too bold. "Wanna try it?" Jack asked, hoping to sound playful and teasing and not desperate with desire.

Paul snorted and shook his head. "You'll never give up, will you? I think I can handle things by myself."

To dispel the nervous energy in the room, Jack dropped Paul an exaggerated wink. "Well, you could always raid Booker's toy closet if you need that blow-up doll."

"I don't really want a doll." A vein in his throat throbbed. What would he do if Jack put his mouth over it? Slid his tongue along his neck and tasted the man he wanted so badly?

He didn't take the time to think. Surging forward, he gripped Paul's biceps and did exactly what he wanted. Groaning, he opened his mouth over his skin.

Paul didn't respond, but he didn't jerk away either. Taking that as a good sign, he continued to explore, pressing kisses over Paul's square jaw to the corner of his mouth.

Breathing heavily, Paul flicked his gaze over Jack. Heat curled around the base of Jack's spine. Dammit, he must be hallucinating because he could swear Paul's eyes burned with interest.

He started to pull back, and Paul held him with a hand on his nape.

"Jesus, man." Jack's throat worked. After all this time, would he get what he'd been asking for?

They stared at each other for five full heartbeats.

Paul's gaze ticked down to Jack's mouth, and his cock swelled with instant need. Resisting the urge to rock his erection into his friend's body, Jack held his breath. He'd made his move. Now he had to let Paul follow through.

A new electricity seemed to vibrate the air between them. Paul didn't move away, and Jack didn't throw himself at him. Just when he believed they were at a standoff, Paul eased his finger across Jack's neck.

Everything inside Jack was whooping with joy and doing a jig. Too well he knew how his advances scared Paul away. Maybe the man needed to go at his own pace.

Heart pounding, he used every ounce of control he had to keep from slamming his mouth over Paul's. When the silence stretched and his boxers wouldn't give around his erection anymore, Jack spoke. "If you don't want a doll, what do you want?"

Paul's gaze zeroed in on his mouth as if it was the sun and he a man who had spent a lifetime in the dark. Jack's throat closed off completely as he struggled with want and need and—dammit—love.

Shit. He was in the same place Riggs had been in months before. Hugh had eventually given in. Paul might too.

"Jack?" Paul's voice was strained.

"Yeah?"

"Shut up." He lowered his head inch by mind-wrecking inch, and *made* Jack shut up.

* * * * *

Paul slanted his mouth over Jack's, tasting man and coffee and a trace of something sweet and feminine—Lissy.

He reeled from Jack's flavors and his own actions. His logical brain wanted to stop and analyze what he was doing and why, but he shoved those thoughts away and just let himself feel.

Dark, forbidden flavors met his tongue as he probed Jack's mouth. The man groaned and swayed against Paul. Their bodies came together, muscle and bone. He could never consider letting another man touch him, but Jack was safe. He might push Paul's boundaries, but he always stopped when asked.

Jack remained still, allowing Paul to explore. Was this what he'd been missing? Because it felt good. No, *great*.

The noise of an ATV engine roaring past the bunkhouse yanked Paul back into reality. He tore his mouth away and released Jack. The man stumbled a step, eyes on fire.

"Paul—"

He shouldn't have kissed him. Now Jack would never leave him alone.

Did Paul want him to?

Hell, he was a wreck and all because he had a week off. That had to be the reason he was losing his mind and entertaining thoughts of having more with his best friend.

How to explain away the strange jelly-like feeling in his chest, though?

"You'd better get back to Lissy. You don't want to keep a woman like her waiting. Someone else will snatch her up."

Jack's eyes cleared, but a crease appeared between his brows. "Yeah, I will. But..."

It was the second time he'd dismissed Jack after a kiss, but he didn't know how to cope right now.

Turning away, Paul fought to make sense of what had just happened—what he'd done. He dropped to the bunk, and the springs groaned. With his face in his hands, he was able to avoid that sad-eyed look Jack often threw him.

The sound of rustling cloth told him Jack was donning a shirt and zipping his fly. Paul didn't look up. Hell, he couldn't trust himself to.

As Jack passed Paul's bunk, he clamped a hand on Paul's shoulder. "I'll be in the barn for a while if anyone needs me."

"'kay." Paul scrubbed his hands over his face.

As Jack left the bunkhouse, Paul wished like hell he knew what to do with the stabbing feeling that kept him from drawing a full breath.

Chapter Five

Paul took a few minutes to collect himself before he tucked the stolen file under his arm and headed out of the bunkhouse. He had no idea what the hell to do about Jack. He wasn't going to make excuses for kissing the man, but he wasn't quite sure if he wanted it to happen again.

All he knew right now was that it wasn't right for him to keep Lissy's file and obsess over a woman he didn't have access to. From what he guessed after speaking with Jack, Lissy was very satisfied with her Boot Knocker.

That meant Paul would never be called in to replace Jack.

As he rounded the corner of the office building, he jerked to a stop. Soft moans met his ears, and even softer voices.

Feminine voices.

Damn, there was only one way into the office, and he'd have to interrupt whatever tryst was taking place.

He pivoted on his heel and skedaddled back to the bunkhouse. He stashed the file under his pillow again. On second thought, Jack had been pretty interested in what was under his pillow. So Paul moved the file to his bottom drawer under his work jeans.

This time as he reached the office building, he strained to hear those moans from earlier. When only the low soughing noise of the wind reached him, he rounded the corner.

And came face-to-face with Holly and Siri, their resident makeover artist. They were leaning against the wood of the outside, Siri's short blue skirt was rucked up to her hips, and Holly's fingers were buried in her pussy. Pale curls peeked between Holly's fingers, and Siri's mouth was opened on a silent groan.

So that's Siri's natural hair color.

Slowly backing away before he was seen, Paul shook his head then went in the opposite direction. Seeing some pussy had him rigid with need again. And with Jack's—and Lissy's—flavors still hot on his tongue, he ached.

"Hey, Paul!"

Still flustered, he stared unseeingly at the green expanse of the distance before he spotted Jack jogging toward him.

One glance and Jack narrowed his eyes. "I forgot to talk to you about the herd. Besides them being fed on grass, what if we start them on some milo and oats…" He trailed off. "You okay, man? If this is about what happened in the bunkhouse—"

"It's not that."

Jack snorted. "Bullshit. Talk to me."

Paul met his friend's gaze, and lowering his head, he leaned close to Jack. "I just saw Siri's bush."

Jack rocked back on his heels. "What?"

"Siri. You know, makeover guru?"

"Yeah, body on fire. She showed you her pussy? You got action from *Siri*?" Jack's eyes were wide. No one had tapped Siri in all their years at the ranch. She politely refused them all, and now Paul knew why.

"No, that's not what I said. I said I saw her bush. And it's not blue like her hair."

Jack released a whoop that echoed across the valley. Paul cracked up laughing. Their shared laughter cancelled all weirdness between them.

"So who was she with? Who's the lucky bastard?"

"It's not a bastard at all. Siri obviously isn't interested in any of us because she's into women."

"You mean..." Jack's eyes registered everything in a heartbeat. "Holly! It's gotta be Holly."

"It was."

Jack shoved Paul in the shoulder, letting out another holler. "Dammit, you're always in the right place at the right time!"

Jack was the lucky son of a bitch with exclusive access to Lissy's bed.

"You saw them going at it?"

Paul nodded.

"*Damn.* Wait'll the other guys hear."

"I'm not sharing it with anyone else. What Holly and Siri do on their own time is their business. And if Siri wanted everyone to know she's a true blonde, she would let her blue hair grow out." Though it suited her so well, Paul couldn't imagine her having any other color.

Again, he and Jack shared a laugh. Jack clapped him on the back. "I'm glad you told me, if no one else. I'm heading to see what horses are available today."

"Going riding with Lissy?"

"Yeah, I wanted to take her to see the herd. She's an experienced rider."

"I know." Too late Paul realized his slip when Jack drew his eyebrows together. "I mean, she mentioned it in the audition. She said she's a show jumper."

"Oh, yeah. Guess that audition is sort of fuzzy in my memory."

What did he mean by that? He didn't give a damn about Lissy? She was just another girl? Trying to play it cool, Paul walked with his friend to the barn. "Why's that?"

"Well..." Jack didn't reply for a long minute. Just when Paul didn't think he'd get another syllable about the topic, Jack spoke. "She sort of threw me for a loop."

They reached the barn but didn't enter. "What's that mean?" Paul asked.

"I'm not sure how to say it." He dragged in a long breath and took even longer to release it. Paul waited, jaw clenched. Finally Jack said, "She really does it for me—turns me on. The attraction is there, and it's not always so strong with some girls, you know?"

Yeah, he knew, and he felt the same thing for the same damn woman. Bobbing his head in answer, he avoided Jack's gaze. He went to the first horse stall and started checking feed and water. Jack followed him in, continuing with his explanation.

"She's gorgeous, but there's something else that drove me a little crazy when I first saw her."

Paul dumped another scoop of feed into Tuck's horse trough. He wished like hell Jack would go confide to Booker, Stowe or Jeremy. Hell, anyone was better suited to listen, but they were best friends. Of course he'd tell Paul.

"She's so easy to talk to, and her sense of humor is great. I think that's why we fit so well in bed. And the fact that she was totally ready—"

Paul spun and *thunked* Jack on top of his head with the metal scoop.

Surprise claimed his features. "Ow! What the hell'd you do that for?"

Better that Jack was spitting mad than continuing with details of how tight Lissy was. Hell, Paul's balls were about to burst from the mere thought.

"Boot Knockers don't kiss and tell." They both knew what bullshit that was. They were single guys making daily conquests. It was impossible to keep all that fun to themselves.

Rubbing his head, Jack said, "Yeah..." He watched Paul feed three more horses before moving off down the line. He talked quietly to a horse for a few minutes, and then returned to Paul.

"I'm laying dibs on Polly for Lissy's mount this afternoon. If anyone asks you—"

"Yeah, yeah, I'll tell him." Paul scooped more grain into another trough. When Jack didn't leave, Paul met his gaze. He let it slither away. Fact was, he was damn jealous of the man.

Besides having Lissy to himself, Jack was so confident. He didn't try too hard to make people like him—he didn't care. His personality lured people to him, where Paul had to fight for every friendship. And Jack was comfortable in his sexuality in a way Paul never would be.

That kiss had shaken Paul up, for sure.

"You have a beef with me, man?" Jack's voice was low.

"'Course not."

"But earlier—"

"We'll talk about that another time. Now get your pansy ass back to Bungalow 15. You've got work to do, and so do I."

Jack cracked a grin, his old self once again. "Good thing it doesn't feel like work." As he passed, Jack squeezed Paul's shoulder.

While Jack went off to Lissy, Paul was left alone. He finished feeding the horses and then dragged the hose down the center of the big, open barn, providing water. Next he mucked out the soiled hay. The hay in the empty stall was tamped down, so he replaced it too.

Finally, he tottered around the supply room, checking on medicines and minerals they gave to a few of the horses. When he could waste no more time in the barn, he reluctantly went outside.

Face tipped up to the sun, he gauged it to be past eleven. Brunch would be on, and Paul's stomach snarled at the thought. Cook's spare ribs were one of his favorites. He'd head over there in a few minutes. Maybe there was something else to be done that he'd forgotten.

You're just trying to put yourself in Lissy's path.

The realization struck him from nowhere, but he knew it to be true. He wanted to have her blazing blue eyes centered on him when she came in after the horse.

He'd heard her speak in the auditorium, but he couldn't help but wish she'd give him a few words to carry him through his long week. Her clear voice held some raspy notes, but she'd also been a little breathless onstage.

Fuck, to have her breathless under him…

And tangling tongues with his best friend had thrown him for a hell of a loop.

He took off for the bunkhouse. Even when Lissy came to the barn, she'd be accompanied by Jack. As soon as Jack saw how Paul acted around Lissy, he'd recognize it for what it was—lust.

Paul couldn't take a chance that Jack would taunt him later. Or worse, that he'd ask him to join them in the bedroom.

If faced with the decision, Paul couldn't trust himself not to agree, and that would put Jack in bed with him. After their kiss, he wasn't sure if it would bother him anymore.

Confused as hell and ignoring the rumblings of his stomach, he strode to the shed. Minutes later he was zooming across the ranch on an ATV. After Hugh and Riggs had fallen for Sybill, they'd built themselves a larger version of the bungalows. The sprawling structure stood alone against the backdrop of field and sky.

Heat waves shimmied in the air, and Paul cut the engine. Swiping sweat from his brow, he could see why Riggs would be a little desperate to get their A/C working.

Hearing the engine, Riggs came outside to meet him. Paul tensed. He and Riggs had a long history of being at odds.

Riggs came forward with a tentative smile, hand extended. Paul clasped it and his shoulders relaxed.

"Hugh said you were coming up. We appreciate it."

"I'm sure you do. Must be ninety already today."

Riggs led the way around the back of the home. The troublesome unit was in pieces, and Riggs's toolbox lay open. He cupped his hand around his nape and rubbed. "I can't find the problem. Since you worked on the units in the bungalows I thought you'd have a good idea."

Paul crouched and assessed the parts on the ground. "Have you checked the thermostat?"

"Yep. I replaced it straight off, since I thought that might be the problem."

Paul grunted and poked at the wiring. "Sometimes it's the wiring."

"It worked for a few days."

"Yeah, it happens. Let me take a look." He prostrated himself on the ground to dig around at the base of the unit where it was wired. Riggs's shadow fell over him, and he welcomed the shade.

After a minute, Riggs asked, "What do you think?"

"Could be a blocked return. It looks as if this outside fan is working."

"It spins all day, but the damn house never gets cool."

Paul peered up at him. "I'm sure that's a hardship."

Riggs gave a short laugh. "You would be correct."

Rolling to a sitting position, Paul wiped his hands on his jeans. "Can I get a look inside?"

"Sure." The house was slightly cooler, but the glass of iced tea Riggs handed him hit the spot. Paul chugged it, and the liquid seemed to seep from his pores. Sweat coated him.

"I often think we should close the ranch for a month during the worst of summer," Riggs said, sipping his own tea.

"I don't think the guys would agree. There would be a mutiny from all that sexual tension."

"You're right. Half of them would be arrested."

They shared a laugh.

"They could always turn to each other," Riggs said, then froze as he obviously remembered who he was speaking to.

Paul waved a hand. "Don't worry about it. I'm used to it."

"Yeah, with Jack as a friend, no doubt." He set his glass in the sink, and Paul drained the last drops from his. "I'm glad you made peace with that. I like you better when we're not beating the piss out of each other."

"It's hard to avoid on this ranch, and...I'm getting used to it." Paul repeated himself as though he'd decided it was true. Riggs arched a brow as if prepared to listen, but Paul didn't know if he wanted to talk. After his actions today with Jack, he felt as if he'd been kicked by a horse and was still rolling.

He met Riggs's gaze. If anyone knew his situation, it was him.

"Some things have been happening."

"Yeah?"

"With me and Jack."

Riggs kept his expression neutral. No judging, just friendship. Paul barreled forward.

"Lately when he makes his advances, I'm not feeling so defensive."

"You guys are good friends. It makes sense."

"Is that how it happened with you and Hugh?"

"Well" — he chuckled — "we landed in bed with a client first and the friendship came later. Trust is pretty important, though, and I think you're figuring that out."

"Yeah." He trusted Jack with his life; they shared laughs and responsibilities. But was he willing to share more?

"Jack's one of the best men I've ever known."

Paul eyed him. The man had been in bed with Jack plenty of times before becoming exclusive with Hugh and Sybill.

Seeming to realize what Paul was thinking, Riggs laughed. "Yeah, he's pretty damn good in bed too. But you know what I mean."

"I do." Tingles radiated through Paul's groin. The way they'd kissed…that had felt better than anything he'd experienced in a long time.

Shaking himself, he said, "I'll take a look at that duct now."

As Paul disassembled the housing around the duct, they talked about the ranch and operations. Hugh was away today with Sybill at auction, looking at a horse they might want to add to their growing herd.

When the conversation flowed back to the ranch and this week's group of women, they joked about Booker's toy collection and who would try to steal a few from his stash.

Paul let a piece of metal clatter to the floor and poked around further. "I heard a couple of the guys talking about playing a joke on Ty this week."

"Yeah? What's that?" Riggs leaned against the wall.

Applying pressure to a certain moveable part, Paul grunted. "They're talking about waxing him."

Riggs hooted with laughter. Ty was one of the few guys on the ranch who liked to keep his body hair. He groomed, but a few guys ribbed him about how big his dick would look if he'd wax.

The part gave way, and Paul banged his knuckle. He cursed but didn't bother looking at the injury. He fiddled with the duct some more.

"How do they plan to wax him?"

"Hold him down, I guess."

"They're asking for a fight. This had to be Jack's idea."

"Far as I know, it wasn't. Besides, Jack is pretty occupied with his woman this week."

Riggs released a low whistle. "Really? I haven't seen him caught up with anyone but you for a long time."

Paul met Riggs's dark gaze.

"Seems he's hung up on you, but maybe this girl is giving you some competition."

Paul looked away.

Riggs made a noise that made Paul glance his direction again.

"What?"

"You've come a long way, Paul."

Ignoring Riggs, he said, "Here's your problem. The heat transfer isn't taking place, and it's tripping your safety overload."

"Do you know how to fix it?"

Glad to be off the subject of Jack, Paul nodded. "It will require a drive into town for some parts, but I'll go now."

"I'm about to head to the grub house. Want to grab lunch before you head out?"

The thought of walking into that grub house and seeing Jack and Lissy cozied up together made him grind his teeth. Besides, he wasn't quite ready to have that talk with Jack yet, and the more he saw him, the better the chance Jack would force the conversation. "Nah. I'll get a burger in town."

"And miss Cook's spare ribs?"

Paul walked through the house, noting the small details that made it a home rather than a bungalow. A stack of laundry on the kitchen table—jeans and western shirts mixed with lacy underthings. And a photo of Hugh, Riggs and Sybill taken at one of the last big rodeos to pass through their area.

Feeling like an intruder, he hurried outside and hopped on the ATV again. Riggs waved as he took off for the main ranch. He had to get rid of Lissy's file when he finished fixing the A/C unit. He couldn't waste another second wishing for something that could never happen.

* * * * *

As Lissy's mount crested the ridge, she let the reins go slack. The view stole her breath. Jack eased his horse so close to hers that her thigh brushed his. Goosebumps broke out on her arms.

"It's gorgeous up here." Did her quiet tone even belong to her?

Jack nodded, a soft smile playing around his lips. "I often thought it would be a perfect place to build a house."

Lissy's imagination erected the walls and placed a red roof on them, matching the others in the valley and the big house farther off. Staring at the big, open sky and the sun that looked so close she could touch it, she nodded. "It would be an amazing location for a house."

Jack used his rough finger to hook her under the jaw.

His intense expression heated her from the inside out. That familiar sensation rose inside her—like a kettle set to boil. Her panties grew damp, and her nipples were sharp points under her thin tank top.

That dark look she'd seen several times over the past hours seized all rational thought, and she even forgot about the breathtaking land.

He tugged on her reins, and Polly danced a little closer, gently crushing Lissy's thigh against Jack's.

"Ready for a gallop? I think you'll like this route," he drawled.

Those goose bumps on her arms spread over her entire body, and somehow she managed a nod.

With a grin that would melt the panties off even the old headmistress at her all-girls' school, Jack dug his heels into his horse. "Yaw!"

He only got a neck's length ahead of Lissy before her competitive nature kicked in. She set her heels into Polly's sides and raced after him. The roll and release of the horse's muscles were as familiar to her as drawing air. She lost herself to the rhythm of hooves.

And the view of Jack's solid back and hard ass bouncing in his saddle weren't too shabby either.

Smiling, she pushed her horse. Lissy's mount back home could have outstripped Jack's in a blink, but she didn't know how far Polly could go. When Jack's horse was a whole body-length ahead of her, Lissy scanned the lay of the land, trying to think of an advantage.

They cut across the field, riding what felt like a mile alongside a fence that enclosed a herd of beef cows. Lissy tried not to gawk at the adorable faces of the calves and focused on winning.

As they circled a small ridge, she took her chance. While Jack went around and then up, Lissy directed her horse up the slope. With a glance over her shoulder, she gauged Jack's speed. If she jumped Polly and landed too close to him, it could be disastrous for all.

Timing was everything, and Lissy had relied on her sixth sense with horses all her life. The hoof beats filled her mind. Five, four, three...

She spurred Polly up and over. The horse's body extended, arcing. Exhilaration sang in Lissy's veins. Being out here, playing cat and mouse with Jack, was a memory she'd tuck away deep in her heart.

When she landed in front of him, he let out a whoop. Laughter bubbled up, and she released it. With a look tossed over her shoulder, she hunkered close to her horse and spurred her on.

Around another bend, and they faced what looked to be hundreds of acres of prime land. Lissy's mind raced ahead, drinking in each blade of grass as well as the little creek burbling in the valley below.

Up here she felt alive in a brand-new way.

Jack galloped hard and pulled even with her. When he reached for her reins, she shook her head. Her entire life had been a competition, and she wasn't about to give him an advantage out here.

In the bedroom was another story.

"Have it your way," he called. His eyes sparked as he set his heels into his horse. The animal lowered its head and raced forward.

Lissy streaked behind, inwardly cursing Jack for giving her a slower mount. Again, she scoured the landscape, looking for a shortcut— a way to gain ground.

The land funneled into a narrow track between two stands of trees running along a ridge. If she could somehow find a way to the other side of that narrowed area, she might reach the spot before him.

"C'mon, Polly. C'mon, girl!" The horse was healthy and strong, and Lissy was certain that with some coaxing, the animal could beat Jack's.

He was three strides ahead of her.

Taking a chance, Lissy veered left. She dipped downhill, and Polly made up some precious ground. As she was working less, Jack's horse was moving up a slope. With any luck, Lissy's idea would give Polly enough of a break that she'd conserve energy.

Sky and land, brown and green, intense blue and the scents of crushed grass. Her breathing kept time with Polly's hooves. As she gave the horse her head and allowed her to pick her best route down the hill, Lissy tethered herself to the moment.

The best race of her life was taking place right now. At the end, she wouldn't be presented a ribbon. If she won, she'd have Jack.

If she lost, she'd have him too.

A wicked grin curved her lips up as she regained control of Polly. "Yawww!" she whooped, guiding the horse hard and fast up the slope.

They burst through the trees and into the funnel. Lissy wheeled around and looked up just as Jack barreled toward her.

Surprise crossed his face, and the closer he came, the faster Lissy's heart pounded. She reined up Polly, and a second later Jack skidded to a stop beside her.

"You're gonna pay for that, woman." He leaped off his horse and landed easily on his feet.

As he stalked toward her, his eyes appeared black. Lissy's pussy squeezed, and more juices wet her panties. She released the reins.

Jack hooked an arm around her waist and yanked her into his arms. They tumbled back into the high grass with Lissy sprawled over his hard body. Muscled biceps flexed as he brought his arms around her.

He rolled her beneath him, pinning her thighs with his, his boots locked atop hers. When he gyrated his hips, letting her feel each fraction of his erection, she moaned.

Lightly pinching her nipple, he stared into her eyes. She reached up and knocked his hat off, needing to dig her fingers into his thick hair. "That was awfully clever of you to take the low ground."

She couldn't resist a smile. "Yeah, I'm awesome that way."

A chuckle rumbled his chest, vibrating hers too. He pinched her nipple lightly, and she moaned at the sensation.

Man, earth and sky. The whole world was perfect at this moment.

When their gazes locked, it was a meteor shower. For long, breathless seconds she lost herself in Jack. Then he swooped in and stole her mind with his kiss.

The heated press of his lips ignited her. She opened to his tongue invasion, and he took total advantage. Slanting his tongue over hers again and again while grinding his erection into the V of her legs.

Low, throaty sounds filled her ears, and she realized she was making the noises. She flung her arms around his back and dragged him closer.

"Hell, baby," he grated out, sounding as affected as she was. But that couldn't be true.

He did this all the time and she was just another girl.

But the way he kissed her felt as if she meant something.

He planted his knee between her thighs, and she ground wantonly against it. While she sought to ease her burning need, he pulled off her top and sports bra. The hot breeze caressed her skin a split second before his fingers did.

Passion flared bright in her as he pressed kisses down her throat to her breasts. She shoved her fingers through his hair and threw herself into the moment. No more thinking about past women in Jack's life. He was with her here and now — it was why she'd come to the ranch.

Reaching between his shoulder blades, she pinched the fabric of his T-shirt and hauled it over his head. God, she loved his body. He was tanned by the sun — everywhere.

She ran her hands over the bulges of his shoulders to his pecs. They were steely and devoid of chest hair. She wanted to rub herself all over him.

When he pinched her nipple hard, she gasped. Tingles rushed to every nerve in her body, and she rocked into his knee more determinedly.

"You want this?" He took her hand and placed it on his rigid cock.

"Yes," she gasped.

His breathing grew harsh as he stared down at her. Then he dipped his head and clamped his lips around her nipple. The dark pull of his mouth on her flesh almost sent her over the edge. Damn, she was so close. A single flick of his thumb over her clit and she'd be sailing.

She found his waistband and opened his fly. With a mewl of need, she ran her fingers down the length of his erection through the barrier of his underwear. Somehow the cotton made him feel harder, hotter. She moaned again.

"Jesus, Lissy, I can't last if you keep making those noises." He rolled off her and yanked off his boots. She kicked hers off too, and in seconds they were both bare under the sky.

His eyes burned like two blue-green flames as he took her hand and drew her to a stand. "We've been to the bedroom rodeo and done the shower two-step a lot, but I need to have you in the place I call home." He swept an arm, indicating the gorgeous landscape.

"Don't forget the barn dance," she said, twining her fingers with his. Her heart beat so fast, she couldn't begin to calm herself. Each time Jack took her, she couldn't imagine it being better. This moment was the best yet.

Jittery with nerves and desire, she let him pull her into his arms. His skin seared hers, and she couldn't stop herself from wiggling against him. He cupped her face as if she was the most precious thing in the world and captured her lips.

The universe faded, and it was only Jack. Emotion bubbled in her throat, and she savored every flip of his tongue.

When he slid down her body to his knees, she stopped breathing. Unable to look away, she watched as he snaked his tongue out and over her pussy lips. Throwing her head back to the sky, she drowned in sensation.

He parted her lips with his tongue, delving into the juicy inner folds. She cried out and her muscles suddenly felt weak. She stiffened her legs, concentrating on staying upright.

But he did his best to try to make her collapse. He danced his tongue down her seam to her opening, then back up, circling her straining nubbin until she thought she'd fall over.

Using the point of his tongue, he ground her clit into her body. Pulsations began deep in her core. She'd never been so orgasmic on her own, but Jack drove her to new heights each time he touched her.

She focused on an inner point that was about to be shaken apart. He licked, lapped, swirled, laved and fucked her with his tongue. The breeze whispered through the trees on each side of them and ruffled his hair. She twisted her fingers in it and bucked against his talented mouth.

"Mmm," he groaned, following the seam down to her soaking channel again.

A single shallow tongue thrust, and she was there—flying. Waves of release claimed her sanity, and she pushed out a guttural sound. He trapped her clit under his thumb, grinding it under the callus and sending her upward again.

Her whole body jerked in time to her pulsations. Cream squeezed from her folds, and he gathered it with eager noises.

When he eased the pressure of his thumb and tongue, she quaked, her knees jelly.

He nuzzled her inner thigh. It took a second for her to bring him into focus—her mind was so hazy. When his intense stare met hers, her heartstrings didn't just tug—they *twanged*. Her whole body reacted to this cowboy who was only hers for a few more days.

"Jack," she whispered.

He made a show of licking his lips that sent lust pounding through her again. His erection bobbed against his carved abs. Slowly he reached for his jeans a foot away. After rummaging through the pockets, he came out with a condom.

"See what you do to me? I don't know if I've ever been this hard, Lissy."

He probably said that to all the women, but she didn't care. Coming from him, it sounded erotic as hell.

He stood, and she reached for him. "Let me put it on you." She'd had one fumbling attempt to slide the rubber on his cock before, and she wanted to perfect the move.

Nodding, he put it in her hand. She tore open the packet and fitted the condom over his swollen tip. It leaked pre-come, and she couldn't resist licking her lips.

Jack groaned. Fired by his reaction, she rolled the condom on with enthusiasm. When he was encased in the barrier, she chewed her lower lip.

"It looks…uncomfortable."

"Not a bit, baby." With that, he yanked her into his arms. She wrapped her legs around his waist and kissed him.

As he fed her flavors back to her, he walked them into the tree line. When rough bark met her bare spine, she broke away from the kiss.

"We're going to have sex like this…against a tree?"

"I thought you wanted me to use my imagination." He nudged her exposed pussy with the head of his cock.

Moaning, she nodded. Yes, a thousand times yes. She wanted this memory to pack up and take home with her. Her sense of reality made her realize she'd never relive a moment quite like this, but she hoped to find somebody who made her feel like Jack.

As he jerked his hips against hers, burying his erection deep in one thrust, she stared into his bright gaze.

She liked him.

Too much.

He burrowed into her channel a fraction deeper, and she cried out. Locking her ankles behind his back, she used her thigh muscles to fuck him. With a grunt, he cradled her on his arms against the tree, keeping the rough bark from irritating her skin.

She rose and fell on him. Parting her lips on his neck, she sucked his salty skin. He groaned, driving her on. At that moment she discovered something about Jack—he loved necking.

Spattering wild kisses over his throat and jaw, she sank over his cock again. He suddenly stilled, and she raised her head. Her lips felt swollen and her face deliciously scraped by his beard.

Without warning he lifted her. His cock sprang free of her body, and she gasped at the emptiness. In a blink he set her on her feet and spun her. She barely had time to hug the tree before he thrust into her pussy.

"Oh," she cried out.

He drove upward in a way that lifted her on her toes. God, he was so deep. So fucking thick. She couldn't last.

Especially when he eased a hand around her hip. When he locked it on her mound, the tip of his finger settling over her clit, she bucked.

His gritty voice heated her ear. "That's it. Take what you need."

She ground against his cock, letting it tease that tight place inside that no toy had ever reached before. Pushing her hips forward, she rubbed against his finger. Her clit swelled.

"More?" he rasped. Taking her earlobe in his teeth, he tugged it lightly.

"Unf." She squeezed him with her pussy walls and he rewarded her with a groan.

"Like this?" He pinched her outer lips, trapping her throbbing clit. Somehow his not touching her neediest spot sent her out of control. He massaged her lips and in turn, her clit between them.

A ragged noise escaped her. Abandoning all sense of propriety, she swirled her hips in a circle, taking what she wanted—craved.

His thighs tightened against hers, and she knew from his breathing rate that he was close.

Damn, how had she learned so much about him in such a short time?

His shaft penetrated deep. She jerked as the first flames of release consumed her. A primal roar hung in the air as he fucked her hard and fast. When he toggled her clit under his finger, she splintered. Sweet, torturous pulsations shook her.

Faintly she was aware of his teeth on her neck and the soft chafe of hair on his thighs. One of the horses stamped a foot nearby, and a bird flitted in the tree branches.

Jack kissed her neck more gently, pressing a path along her nape, moving her hair with his free hand. When he twisted her hair around his fist and tugged lightly, shocks of sensation raced over her scalp.

He rolled his hips, sinking his still-hard cock into her once more. He pulled her head back until he could capture her lips. Emotion rocked her. In a few days she'd board a flight back to California, where she'd resume her old routine.

Leaving Jack would hurt.

Oh no.

She couldn't afford to get hung up on a rent-a-stud. She'd have to lock away whatever she was feeling and just keep their interactions physical. He was giving her pleasure, nothing more.

As his tongue swept the interior of her mouth, she squeezed her eyes shut. *He's not mine. It's his job.*

She'd have to keep telling herself that.

* * * * *

Jack kept forgetting to feed Lissy. When they were together, he lost track of time. He didn't realize they'd spent most of the afternoon on the ridge until the sun lowered in the sky.

With care he helped her dress, jumped into his clothes too. She watched him pull on his boots and hat, her eyelids heavy with desire.

A lot of women looked at him this way, but it was different with Lissy. She made him feel as though he was the only man on earth.

His heart was full of that strange heat again. It was pointy and sweet all at once, but he couldn't figure out what to make of it. Maybe he was just hungry.

He helped her mount. She gave him a funny look but didn't comment. Hell, she was probably a better rider than he was. She didn't need help into the saddle. He just couldn't quit touching her.

Scrubbing a hand over his face only filled his nose with her decadent scents. He could nearly feel her clit twitching under his finger as she'd come. And her walls contracting around his cock —

He clamped off the emotional artery bleeding these thoughts and swung onto horseback. Together they trotted out of the funnel between trees. This time there was no race to return to the ranch. Though they'd have all the time in the world upon their return, he was reluctant to leave. Having her alone had been so right.

He glanced at her from under his hat brim. Warm brown hair waved back from her face, and her lips were swollen from his kisses. Hell, now he was thinking about her sucking his cock.

She was damn good at it for having no experience. She read his reactions and took advantage. She knew where to press her tongue and when.

His cock lengthened behind his fly, and he shifted in his saddle.

They didn't speak as they passed the herd of cows or descended into the valley. A few figures crossed from a bungalow to the swimming pool. Still more headed toward the grub house.

"Must be dinnertime," he said.

Her expression grew absorbed as if she were searching inwardly for hunger pains. "I guess I could eat."

What day was this? His mind flipped back through the number of times he'd had Lissy come for him, and he could barely figure out when she'd arrived on the ranch. It seemed like ages since he'd led her offstage, yet he felt as if he'd just met her.

"Tonight I think there's enough players to have a football game," he said slowly. Yes, that was right. Football night. They rotated activities at the ranch—cornhole tournament, mud race on ATVs, boot-scootin' with a local band and football. The rodeo was the big finale of every week, though.

Her body rolled with Polly's movements. Everything about her was sensual. Did she know this? Why hadn't some man snapped her up long ago? Idiots, all of them.

"What kind of football?"

"Well"—he grinned—"it's supposed to be flag football, but…you'll see."

"Can I play too?"

He stared at her. The women usually enjoyed watching the Boot Knockers play. By the end of the game, they were hot and bothered. In his years at the ranch, Jack had seen a lot of athletic women, but none had ever asked to play.

Too easily he pictured Lissy streaking down the field with a ball tucked under her arm. Every cowboy would have a boner for her.

He swallowed hard. "We'll see," was all he said.

They got cleaned up and went to the grub house. It was loud with chatter. The long tables were filled with Boot Knockers and their women. He waved at Riggs as he entered.

"How's the unit?"

"Working fine. I appreciate how cool it is in the house."

"I do too," Sybill said with a flush that spelled trouble. Sure enough, Hugh pushed back his chair. It scraped the floor, and several people looked up from their chicken and cornbread. When Hugh picked up Sybill, she squealed, kicking her legs over his bulky arm.

Riggs stood more slowly. He tipped his hat at Jack, and they shared a grin. Without a doubt Hugh, Riggs and Sybill would be taking advantage of the cooler bedroom conditions.

"They look happy." Lissy's observation roused Jack.

"What? Oh yeah." He watched the trio leave. What would it be like to have a connection like theirs? Tied hearts and shared lives?

With a hand on Lissy's lower back, he led her to the buffet along one wall. Booker's voice carried, louder than most. The girl he'd won giggled.

Jack handed Lissy a plate and let her go ahead of him in line. He watched her select her food, curious about her preferences. Not surprisingly she chose a lot of high-energy foods — proteins and vegetables — while steering clear of the cornbread and homemade rolls.

She grabbed a bottle of water from the ice chest and turned to Jack. He dropped another drumstick onto his plate and glanced around for a place to sit. What he wanted was to take her to the ridge again. The next best thing was the outdoor seating.

"C'mon." He jerked his head toward the side door, and she followed him. When he pushed it open with his hip, Lissy's mouth fell open.

Teller had Jeremy pinned to the wall, a hand planted over his head and one on Jeremy's fly. They didn't even look up. Another kind of arousal crept through Jack. While he loved having women—having Lissy—he adored having a man wrapped around him.

"Um, let's try to find a table inside."

Lissy didn't speak as she located a spot in front of the expanse of windows overlooking the ranch. She sat, legs crossed, and ate two broccoli spears before meeting Jack's gaze.

"Is that common here?"

He knew exactly what she was asking but played dumb. "What do you mean?"

She flicked her jaw toward the door. "*That.* Two guys?"

"Well…yeah. Some like it." *Some like me.* He'd never made excuses about his sexuality a day in his life, but for some reason he was hesitant to admit it to Lissy.

She nibbled a bite of chicken on her fork then lowered it. "But what about their women?"

He chugged some sweet tea. Backhanding his mouth, he said, "What about them?"

"Do the guys ignore the girls and go with each other?"

"Not exactly. Sometimes they seek each other out during their free time. We couldn't possibly ignore our ladies." He winked as his cock extended along his inner thigh. "And some of the women want more."

Jack watched with fascination as Lissy's face mottled red. The color crept up her face and disappeared into her hairline. Even the tops of her breasts peeking from her blue tank top were pink.

She leaned across the table and lowered her voice. "You mean they want two men?"

"Yeah."

"Have you…?"

He met her gaze fully. "Yes."

She turned so red it was almost painful to look at. A dew of perspiration broke out on her throat. Glancing around the packed room, she asked, "Who have you been with in here?"

"Uh…" He didn't like the way this conversation was going. If she was against male/male relations, she might request a different Boot Knocker. Of course, they all interacted with men.

All but one.

"Have you been with him?" She cut her eyes to the side, and he followed her gaze.

Jesus. Paul stared at them. He'd placed his hat on the table beside him, and his hair was rumpled in that way Jack loved. Of all the guys for Lissy to ask about.

"No," Jack said immediately.

"Why not? You don't like him?"

Jack fought to keep from squirming. "I like him fine. He's my best friend."

Lissy's blue eyes widened. "Oh." She looked between Jack and Paul then returned her attention to her plate. Maybe she'd drop the subject now.

After another bite of chicken, she glanced at Paul again. A very pretty blush coated her cheeks. Jack let his fork clatter to his plate. Fuck, she was attracted to Paul.

Well, who wasn't? His rugged jawline drew Jack like a horse to water. Not to mention that chest. And ass.

Shhhhit.

Lissy ate another bite. Paul gaped at her, and Jack swung his head toward his friend. In a heartbeat he translated Paul's expression.

He wanted Lissy too.

Dark heat rocketed through Jack. He'd get them both in bed and blow both of their minds. He'd—

No, he wouldn't. Paul didn't accept invitations for threesomes.

Lissy's voice came slow and unnaturally quiet. "You like him."

Ripping his attention from Paul, he centered on Lissy. Her eyes couldn't get wider, and that gorgeous pink hue in her cheeks drove him crazy.

Was there any point in denying his attraction to Paul? Everyone on the ranch knew Jack had tried to get into Paul's Wranglers more times than he could count. There wasn't any harm in admitting this to Lissy, especially since she seemed to be turned on.

"I do," he said, biting into drumstick. Spiced meat filled his mouth, and he chewed.

Lissy returned to her food too, and Paul got up to leave. He took his time gathering his tray and setting his hat on his head just so. He shot Lissy another lingering look before pivoting to leave.

"Football game's starting in half an hour," someone called.

Jack raised a brow at Lissy. The tension between them dissipated with one beautiful smile from her. They finished eating and he told her tidbits about a few of the Boot Knockers nearby. She still seemed fixated most on Paul, asking a few more questions about him and chewing her lower lip. Jack cleared both of their trays and tangled his fingers with hers to lead her outside. Football games usually took place behind Bungalows 11 through 15. The wide space was one of the driest spots on the ranch, and no animals left surprises on the ground for them to fall into.

When they reached the field, a few people were seated on the sidelines. Women leaned back on their palms, looking more at ease than they had in the auditorium earlier that week.

Of course, they'd had a lot of reason to relax in the past few days.

Jack grinned.

He stroked his thumb over Lissy's silky palm and watched her hair tease her jawline. Leaning close, he kissed a particularly sensitive spot below her ear. When she shivered, his head swelled a little.

Especially since Paul was looking. His friend shook his head as if warding off an annoying fly.

As Holly took the field, a cheer went up. He caught Paul's eye again, and they shared a smirk, knowing Holly had been tapping Siri.

"Who's ready to play ball?" she shouted.

"Whoooeeee!" several cowboys hooted.

Holly held up a football, and more hoots resounded across the field.

"You didn't say whether I'm allowed to play or not," Lissy said, turning to Jack.

"We'll see if you really want to in a minute."

Holly spiked the ball, and the guys rushed the field. There, they reached for their boots. Ten boots were flung at the sidelines, and some girls got up and placed them neatly.

Socks followed. And more boots.

"They play barefoot?" Lissy asked.

Jack hitched his foot up and yanked off one boot then the other. He dropped his socks then reached for his belt buckle.

Lissy's mouth fell open and she swept a look over the field, where the other guys were stripping down to their undies for the game.

"Still wanna play?" he asked.

"Hell, yes." She reached for her shirt hem.

* * * * *

The moment Lissy started taking off her clothes, Paul's nerves went a little haywire. His heart pounded so hard he felt a little dizzy. Especially when her tanned, lean midriff appeared. She twisted and turned to pull off her own cowgirl boots. Watching her shimmy out of her jeans was the hottest thing he'd seen in his life.

He didn't often play in this game, not loving the contact with the other guys in their underwear. Occasionally he participated to get his woman fired up for later, and it had worked well.

His only excuse for pulling off his T-shirt and working on his button fly was temporary insanity. Otherwise known as Lissy.

"Holy hell, Paul's going out," Ty shouted to the others.

Jack whirled around mid-step. A strange look fluttered across his features.

Paul didn't care. What mattered was Lissy was staring at him. Her blue eyes intense, her ripe lips parted slightly. Damn, to know how she tasted...

He kicked the mass of his clothes and boots into a pile and hit the field running. Then it was on. Flags were attached to underwear. The ball was clutched between Jack's muscled thighs before he set it on the ground.

"Ready, man?" Jack called, that damn flirtatious crooked smile unmistakable. Paul had seen it often enough.

Paul attached his flag so it could be yanked off easily. Sometimes the guys got overzealous and ripped whatever cloth they got hold of.

The grass felt good on his bare feet, and he couldn't think why he didn't go without boots more often. He skirted the group and took his position on the team opposing Jack's.

Lissy jogged onto the field, and everyone went crazy. Loud shouts and sexual innuendos flew. Paul clenched his teeth against the urge to shut them all up, but she seemed at ease.

In her cotton boyshort panties and sports bra, she stole Paul's mind. She was gorgeous and confident in her own skin. And what fine skin it was too.

Her legs were sleek and toned, her ass high and tight. And the way her breasts rode beneath the fabric of her bra was enticing as hell.

His cock twitched along his abs.

She smiled, and his breath hitched. When she took her place behind Jack, hands cupping the air in preparation to catch the ball, Paul couldn't take his eyes off her.

Jack said something over his shoulder, and she laughed. Paul smiled in response. Jack faced forward and winked right at Paul. Awareness penetrated his entire being.

"Hike!"

The ball flew into Lissy's hands, and she was running. Lithe body streaking down the field, right toward Paul.

Adrenaline rushing, he charged her. As she breezed past him, his fingers grazed the flag on her hip.

Along with a length of smooth thigh.

Aching with need, he sprinted after her. Two other guys came at her from other angles, but damn, she was fast.

Paul lunged for her, hit the ground and rolled. He came up with a bigger erection than before. Jack hollered at him from across the field just as Lissy ran into the end zone.

Another half-naked female whizzed by Paul and made a grab at his flag. He laughed at her antics as she rushed into Jeremy's arms. He spun her.

Lissy did a touchdown dance, complete with wiggling ass and shaking breasts.

More women piled onto the field. If Paul thought their games intense before, it was nothing compared to this one.

As Lissy jogged past him, she graced him with a heart-throbbing smile. He watched her go right into Jack's arms. He looked directly at Paul when he angled his head and kissed her.

Tearing his gaze away, Paul waited for them to reassemble their formation. After that, he lost himself in the motion of her body—

twists and turns, a leap that sent his pulse racing.

She ran by him, dangerously close. Was she taunting him? In the grub house he'd seen the interest on her face and guessed Jack was filling her in on how many times he'd tried to get Paul in his bed. Maybe...

Paul stopped dead, his feet suddenly like cement.

If Lissy was truly interested, she might request he join them. What then?

His cock leaked a little pre-come, and a wet ring formed on his underwear. Stowe snagged Lissy's flag and held it up with a victory roar.

She laughed good-naturedly but Paul noted the firming of her lips. Jack got her back on his side and gave her a pep talk. They made fists and rapped knuckles. The show of camaraderie was a jab of pins into Paul's psyche.

He'd never seen Jack act this way with anyone else—male or female. It was almost as if he and Lissy were close friends with enough attraction to melt the grass on the field.

Huffing a little with annoyance, Paul took his position.

Lissy's snap count confused the hell out of Paul's team and Holly called them on starting before the ball was in play.

Lissy leaned over Jack and said something to him. He looked up and met Paul's gaze. Across the distance, Paul's internal alarms went off.

Oh no. No, no, no. He wouldn't, couldn't share a bed — or a woman — with Jack.

Could he?

Their kiss in the bunkhouse hadn't seemed forbidden. Actually, it had been exciting and familiar all at once.

Was he ready to examine why he was growing more attracted to Jack?

When he shook himself, Lissy was careening through the players with wild abandon. She skidded near enough to Paul that he could snag her flag, but he fell back and let her pass.

While every bone in his body screamed at him to go after her and claim what he wanted so badly, he walked off the field. Gathering his clothes, he felt her gaze following him. Jack called his name.

But   Paul   kept   walking.

Chapter Six

Blue moonlight fell over Lissy's hair, turning it to silver. After a sweaty game and a sweatier hour in the bungalow, she'd showered and secured it in a long tail. Several times Jack had wrapped his hand around the length, tugging gently and remembering that moment he'd kissed her while she came apart around him.

Sweet Jesus, he was really losing it. He wasn't the type of guy to reminisce about past sex. He was always looking forward to the next tryst.

She tilted her head back to stare at the stars. They blazed across Texas, lighting up the whole universe, but all Jack really saw was Lissy.

Yep, losing it.

He wrapped his arms around her and nuzzled her throat. She smelled like berries and woman. She softened in his embrace, curling against his chest. For a long minute they stood holding each other.

"I've been thinking about what we talked about at dinner, Jack."

Oh no.

"Mm. What's that?" Strands of her hair caught on his unshaven jaw.

"I've grown very comfortable with you in a short time, and I think you have too."

He nodded, rubbing his cheek on her temple. So comfortable that she was shoving him off-balance.

"But when you answered me about that cowboy you said you liked, I don't think you were telling me the whole story."

He drew away enough to look at her eyes. In the moonlight, they glittered black. His chest worked around a sigh that he finally released. "What do you want to know?"

"You said you like him."

"I do like Paul." Man, why did he sound as though he'd just swallowed a bit and a spur and chased it with whiskey?

"He's your friend?"

"Yeah."

"But you've never...had relations with him?"

He tightened his hold on her upper arms. "What are you getting at, baby? What's going on in that pretty little head of yours?" He

192

didn't want to know, yet he craved a certain answer.

She pulled away and stepped back. Two steps, three. She wrapped her arms around her middle, suddenly appearing shy when she never had before. Not even while streaking in her skivvies across a football field with more than a dozen mostly naked cowboys and a few of their women.

He held out his hands, palms up. "Just say it. There's no barrier between us."

She bobbed her head. "You're right. I can tell you anything because I won't be here forever."

Hell, that was right. She was leaving in a few days.

Chest tight, he said, "Just speak your mind. Whatever it is I'll—"

"I wondered if he—Paul—might come to my bungalow."

He stared at her for three long heartbeats. Was she putting him out to pasture? Replacing him with six feet of hunky man with the body of a god?

"I-I mean… Damn, Jack, the way you're looking at me is making me more nervous."

He stepped close to her. "What exactly are you asking?"

"I want Paul to come to our bed." Her voice dropped with every syllable uttered, so the final word was a scant breath.

He let his head fall back and he stared unseeingly at the Big Dipper. When he directed his gaze at her again, she was twisting her hands. He placed his over them to still the movement.

"Lissy. Baby. I want that. Believe me. But it's Paul's week off, and he's taking care of the new herd."

"Oh?"

"I'll talk to him, but maybe you shouldn't get your hopes up about him in particular."

Her shoulders slumped. "I'm not sure I'd want another cowboy."

Jack couldn't stand her disappointment. Maybe that kiss Paul had laid on him had been his way of saying he was ready. But Jack couldn't make that call. Paul had to.

"Hey, if you've got your heart set on it, I'll talk to him."

"You know, I only chose two cowboys from that album — you and him."

Jack swiped both hands over his face.

"And since I know you like him, I thought…"

He ducked his head to capture her gaze. "You thought what?" he prodded.

"Well it would be hot to see you getting pleasure. You know, in that way."

He laughed. He couldn't help it. The idea of being with Paul was so strong and compelling, it brought him joy. Add Lissy to the mix, and he'd probably have heart failure. At least he'd die a happy man.

"I'd benefit from it too," she went on. "Having two amazing cowboys' attention on me would be a fantasy I didn't realize I wanted. After being on that field with him and you today, I couldn't help but play out the moves in my head."

At her words he drowned for a long minute. Fuck, yes. Paul moving inside Lissy as Jack moved inside Paul. Lissy sitting on Paul's face while Jack sucked his friend's cock. A half dozen more scenarios and erotic positions flashed through his mind.

He shook his head to clear it.

"Maybe I shouldn't have asked."

Jack cuddled her against his chest. "You definitely should have. I'm glad you did. You've just got to...give me a little time to talk to Paul."

Jack wrapped his arms around her and tried to think of a way to disappoint her.

* * * * *

The herd was happy and well-fed. Riggs's A/C unit was humming like a happy bee. It hadn't rained a drop, which meant the corner of the barn stayed dry.

And Paul was bored as hell.

He leaned against the fence, watching the horses Hugh and Sybill had purchased at auction. Pretty things with long, slender limbs and flowing manes. When paired with some of the stronger stock, they'd produce very desirable offspring.

"I hoped I'd find you here."

Paul swung his head to find Jack approaching. He smiled and rested his elbows on the top rail while his friend took a spot beside him. "How's your week going?"

"Pretty well." Jack stood close, but Paul didn't move away. A good sign.

"Really?" He quirked a brow at Jack. "So well that you're out here instead of holed up with a gorgeous, desirable woman in Bungalow 15?"

For long seconds, he didn't speak. Just leaned on the fence. Paul waited, noting the leaping muscle in the crease of his jaw. It was impossible not to think of their kiss in the bunkhouse.

Jack didn't speak or make a move on Paul, as he expected.

"What happened?" he asked at last.

Jack pushed a sigh through his nose. "I hear Dylan asked you to share that brunette with the great ass."

Paul grimaced. Yeah, he had. Of course he'd turned Dylan down, but he wasn't as defensive and annoyed as he should have been. He was getting way too soft after only a few days alone.

Besides, he couldn't think of Dylan that way. "That's right."

"Hmm." Jack didn't say any more.

One of the horses trotted by, so close Paul could reach out and touch her.

"Did you come all the way out here to ask me about Dylan and the girl with the great ass?" He hadn't even noticed her great ass.

Jack tightened his lips. "No."

"Then say it. Why hold back now?"

When Jack met his gaze, Paul's heart seized. Oh shit. It was going to happen. Lissy wanted a threesome with him and Jack, and how the hell would Paul manage to say no?

Jack nodded. "She wants it."

"Asked for me? Or you're asking for me?"

Jack's throat worked. "Both."

His mind whirled. What did he want? Why was his pulse tripping and why were his jeans growing tight? He'd kissed Jack, and there was no reason for it other than he wanted to taste him — feel him.

But he didn't know if he was ready.

When Paul didn't respond, he went on.

"You know I want you. Hell, it's no secret. And after the kiss in the bunkhouse, I started to wonder if you want me too." He cocked a brow at Paul.

Dropping his gaze was a cowardly thing to do, but Paul couldn't breathe let alone speak. He needed time. He needed —

"Lissy requested you specifically. During the selection process, she only picked two cowboys — you and me."

Running a forefinger along the wooden fence, he picked up a splinter. He folded his fingers into his fist and focused on his friend's words. Though his heart was doing a tango that Lissy had asked for him, how would he react when Jack couldn't keep his hands to himself? Hell, maybe Paul would be the aggressor. He'd taken control of that kiss, after all.

Jack crowded closer, his body strong and solid against Paul's side. His heat permeated Paul's clothes. Paul stared at the blades of grass, a rock and a buzzing fly.

"Why did you kiss me in the bunkhouse?"

Yeah, why? He'd mulled over the same question for long hours, and what it came down to was or months Jack had been a huge part of his life, and that included stolen kisses and caresses. Somewhere along the way Paul had begun to like it.

Paul swooped in and claimed his mouth. He rapped the brim of Jack's hat with his knuckles, shoving it off. Jack locked his arms around Paul.

They grappled for a moment. Paul gripped his shoulder and tugged him close even as Jack latched onto Paul's ass. Plunging his tongue between Jack's lips, Paul gave himself up to his cravings.

Jack smelled like skin warmed in the sun. Paul groaned. The graze of his teeth ignited him further.

"Does this mean you want me?" Jack's smile spread under Paul's lips.

"Dunno what I want. I'm trying to find out. You talk too damn much." He slammed his mouth over Jack's again and pivoted the man, pinning him to the fence with his body.

Jack's bulge pressed against his, and Paul's balls clenched tight. As they kissed, he forgot about analyzing his desires. Maybe no microscope was needed—let hormones take over.

Jack never seemed to think too hard about sex, and that might be the key.

Would Paul lose sight of who he was by letting this threesome happen? Until a few months ago, he'd been a ranch hand and now he was very much desired by a lot of women. Back then, he'd never believed he could kiss or touch a man, yet it felt good. He'd been raised with one set of ideas, but the ranch had forced him to face his own desires.

His fingers found their way under Jack's T-shirt and up the planes of his hard chest.

Jack withdrew from the kiss first, which shocked the hell out of Paul since he was always the one doing the pursuing. Paul leaned back and stared into his eyes. Jack's lips were swollen and damp, his eyelids heavy.

"So you *are* into me."

Paul snorted a laugh. "Maybe a little."

Shaking his head, Jack's smile stretched. "Damn, after all this time."

"Don't get too cocky. It was a few kisses. I didn't say I'm ready to crawl into bed with you."

"I know, but you need to make up your mind right quick. I can't disappoint this woman. I care about her too much, and the thought of seeing her unhappy makes me want to *drag* your ass into that bungalow. I'd do anything to make her happy."

"It has to be me?" Paul met his gaze. Jack held it for a beat too long.

"Tell me you don't *want* it to be you." Jack squeezed Paul's shoulder.

He turned his head slightly, his lips inches from Jack's. The fire inside him was banked, but far from extinguished. "I'll do it."

Jack's eyes flared with shock. "You will?"

"Yeah. But I get her alone first."

* * * * *

Lissy fidgeted, hands twisting as she sat on the step of Bungalow 15. Jack was at her side, his presence solid and comforting. That was confusing enough considering she'd just met the man.

More perplexing was feeling like a young girl waiting for her first date. Paul was due any minute.

Jack slipped an arm around her waist and pulled her against him. His lips were soft against her hair. "I promise he'll treat you right."

"This is insane. What happened to me? Since I booked this trip, I've gone crazy. I never for a minute believed I'd do these things."

"It's a little like going on vacation and getting a tattoo."

"Or deciding to jump out of a plane." Her stomach quivered in the same way she expected it might if she made such a leap.

Jack pressed another kiss to her head. "He's a nice guy."

She met his gaze, that hollow in her belly filling with butterflies. They took flight as her reason for sitting on the stoop struck her. Paul had agreed to her request for a threesome.

Jack's eyes were beautiful, varying shades of blue that twinkled like stars. He squeezed her middle, and she relaxed against him. Bizarre, insane, cuckoo. Whatever she wanted to call it, she'd won the title.

She redirected her attention across the field. The sun was lowering in the sky, tipping the grasses gold. "The land is beautiful."

"Yes, it is. I couldn't live anywhere else."

She nodded. To take Jack out of Texas would be like hooking a rare fish in the ocean and pulling it to the surface, only to put it in a zoo. This man was a hundred percent cowboy, and he belonged here.

She'd lived her entire life in California. Did that hold true for her?

No, she'd traveled enough to realize she could be happy anywhere. While she was close to her parents, she could pull up roots and sink them in another one of the fifty states. Beach volleyball wasn't huge in Texas, but her degree would serve her well in a state full of horse ranches.

"Here he comes." Jack's voice sent a thrill to her belly. It slithered south and took up residence between her thighs.

She saw Paul surrounded by nothing but sky and land. Her breath caught, and she swore Jack stopped breathing. Paul's muscles rolled as he walked. He wore low-slung jeans and a denim shirt, his hat tipped low.

Was it possible for panties to scorch to ash? Because Lissy's might have.

She stood as Paul neared. Jack gained his feet too, anchoring her to his side. His support kept her wobbly knees from giving out.

She turned to Jack. "You know I adore you, right? That you've been perfect?"

His smile was wide, his eyes shining with understanding. "Baby, you don't have to explain. You're here to reach your dreams, and it's all good. I mean, look at him. He's a lot to dream about."

"Yes," she whispered. With her heart satisfied that she wasn't hurting Jack's feelings, she stepped down to meet Paul. Their gazes connected, and her heart did a slow, lazy somersault. Was it possible to be infatuated with two men?

* * * * *

Paul ducked his head a bit to stare into Lissy's eyes. They shined with vitality, just as in the photo in her file. He'd been drawn to her for so many reasons, but her spirit was number one.

"I'm Paul," he said quietly.

"Lissy."

He watched her lips form her name, heat dousing him from boots to hair follicles. He offered his arm, and she threw Jack a glance before wrapping her hand around the crook.

"I'll take her to dinner," he told Jack.

"Good."

"And for a stroll to the barns."

"Sounds good." Jack's mouth quirked with amusement. Paul felt like a kid picking up his date.

He shared so much with Jack. Sharing Lissy with his friend felt like an extension of that. He relaxed and smiled back. "The herd's doing fine, but I know you plan to ride up there."

Tipping his hat, Jack said, "Yes, I do. Have her back by midnight."

Lissy looked between them, and seeing their amusement, released a laugh that dispelled the tension between them all. She pressed Paul's arm. "See you in a while, Jack."

"Enjoy yourself." He dropped her a wink then gave Paul a nod.

Paul set off walking with the woman of his fantasies at his side. He'd told Jack he liked curvy women, but until Lissy, he hadn't realized he had an ideal in mind. She was powerful and comfortable with herself, which was so refreshing.

"Are you hungry?" he asked.

"A little nervous."

He let his gaze roam all over her body and wanted to let his hands wander too. But not yet. He had to do this right, because there wouldn't be second chances. She'd leave in a few days, and he didn't want to look back and have regrets.

"Would you like to walk a little before we get dinner?"

"Yes, please."

Paul steered them away from the grub house and out across an expanse of grass between outbuildings.

"What are all these structures?" Lissy asked.

"Jack didn't show you around?"

A blush was in her voice. "We haven't been outside too much."

"But you rode horses."

"Yes, and it was fantastic. I ride all the time, but it's so open here. We ran for miles."

Paul smiled. Yes, she was a true outdoorswoman. Nothing about Lissy was stuffy. "Did he take you up to where the land funnels?"

"Yes, he did. It's beautiful."

"You should consider yourself lucky, you know."

She started, riveting him in her blue-eyed gaze. "Why lucky?"

As he returned her stare, he realized something besides lust was building inside him. He liked her—a lot. If he'd met her on the street, he would have jogged after her and asked for her number. She'd hooked him and was slowly reeling him in.

"Jack's never taken anyone up to that bit of land, as far as I know."

"Really?"

"Yep."

"But you've been there with him."

"I have. We ride there pretty often during our free time. The terrain's a challenge."

"I loved it. And the solitude."

Paul couldn't stop his smile. "It's one of the things I love about that stretch." He covered her fingers with his free hand. The silky digits felt good under his. She released a low sigh. "I'd like to get your thoughts on another patch of land. Should we change plans? Maybe take a ride?"

He looked over her dark jeans, boots and simple top. She wasn't wearing accessories, which was good because she didn't need adornment. She was perfect as she was.

"I'm always ready to ride." She bounced a little as they neared the barn. Paul watched her without pause as he opened a stall door and she greeted the horse she'd ridden before. It nosed her hand, and she stroked its neck, her face glowing with happiness.

"Want me to saddle her for you?" When their gazes connected, a warm weight settled in his stomach.

"Nah, I've got it."

Her motions as she selected a saddle and strapped it on the horse were poetry. Each movement was economical yet graceful. Everything she did was with purpose.

He readied his mount and led them into the early evening. He fitted his boot in the stirrup just as Lissy swung into her saddle.

She wheeled the horse around, her wild grin stealing Paul's breath. "Let's see what you've got."

Was that a challenge? Because he sure as hell was up for it.

He took off after her, thundering close behind. Her body rose and fell, leaving him with lurid images of her naked and in his bed.

As they galloped across the ranch, Paul pulled ahead of her. Her competitive streak had her pushing faster, though. Feeling light at their play, he veered right. She glanced over her shoulder and had no choice but to speed up to keep abreast of him.

For long minutes he enjoyed the energy snapping between them and the breeze on his face. They cut across a natural dip and slowed to a canter.

He motioned for her to come closer, and she did, hair loose and soft on her shoulders, eyes shining. Reaching out, he caught her reins in one hand and her shoulder in the other. He leaned in his saddle and pulled her right into a kiss.

Hot lust ignited in his groin as he tasted her. Her lips gave way to a gasp, and suddenly his tongue was in her mouth. No awkwardness, just pure harmony.

He ran his tongue along hers, learning her feel and wanting — needing — to take more, but forcing himself to go slow. They were moving fast enough as it was. He couldn't risk scaring her.

Gently, he kneaded her shoulder. The muscle leaped under his fingers, and he took more liberties, threading his fingers into her hair.

As he drank in her tastes, his horse danced away. Instead of letting Lissy go, he dragged her off her mount and across his lap.

She squealed and wrapped her arms around him as he lowered his mouth over hers. Her ass was cradled on his groin, and fuck, he was so hard and throbbing for her. Passion rose inside him, so similar to his feelings when he'd kissed Jack.

Damn, these two were suddenly tangled in his mind. He groaned, tasting her, thinking of him. Dark need ripped through him, and he yanked away before he could ravage her.

She followed him, beautiful face upturned, eyes lidded.

"Hell, I can't stop." He bit at her lips, and when she opened, he sucked her tongue. She clung to him and then kissed him full force.

Until now, he'd never known such craving. She wiggled on his lap and raked at his shoulders with her short nails. He nibbled a path of kisses down her jaw to her throat. She threw her head back, giving him perfect access to the sweet spot behind her ear.

He sucked the tender skin, losing his mind a little. By the time he regained his senses, his cock was a heavy ridge against her ass, and she wore a bright red mark on her neck.

Pulling away, he gazed down at her. She bit into her lower lip, and he couldn't suppress a groan as the flesh plumped around her white teeth.

"That was…whooeee," she murmured.

His mouth quirked up at the corner. "You're turning into a cowgirl right quick."

She hummed a laugh. Her horse circled around them, causing them both to laugh. "Guess I should grab the reins."

"I think you already have." He stared at her until she squirmed. Damn, she was sweet and succulent.

She drew away a little and dragged a breath in. "I feel like a different person here."

"I know the feeling." If someone had told him a year ago that he'd be entertaining the thoughts of sharing a woman with Jack—or even kissing his best friend—he would have given him an earful.

"You look as confused as I feel." She laughed.

"Guess I am. Want to walk a little?"

"Sure." Some women would have waited for him to lower her to the ground but not Lissy. She jumped off and landed with practiced ease.

Grinning, he dismounted too and hobbled his horse so it could graze. Lissy did the same, and then they turned to each other.

She was flushed from their kisses, and damn, he wanted more.

Slow and easy. Give her time.

If he were honest, he needed a little time too. He really was a little confused.

He felt like a cowboy who'd been given his first horse, land and even stars for gazing. He'd had all these things before, but being with Lissy was a special privilege. And Jack was causing another kind of upheaval in his system.

He extended a hand for Lissy, and she slipped hers into it. They walked a short distance in silence, and he reveled in the feel of her hand clasped around his and the little tendrils of hair that played around her face in the breeze.

"When I was little, I thought the sun only hung over Texas."

She laughed, a low, throaty sound that raised the hairs all over his body. "Why did you believe that?"

"Because there's so much land, I thought it took the whole sun to keep it alive."

She nodded. "Makes sense."

"My dad told me I was being silly. He always said I was a dreamer, and I guess he broke me of that early."

She studied him, her eyes tender. "What was wrong with being a dreamer?"

He lifted a shoulder. Not only did he not know why being a dreamer was a bad thing, but he had no clue why he was confiding to Lissy. His family was a raw spot with him.

"My family and I have always been at odds."

"You don't get along with them now?"

"No communication whatsoever."

She laid a hand on his arm. "That must be hard. I can't imagine not having my parents as support. Though I've always been independent, knowing they were encouraging me pushed me to do better."

He smiled. Getting a glimpse into her life was like a warm blanket tossed over his shoulders on a cold day.

"The guys and this ranch have been my family for a while now. Even before I became a Boot Knocker, I was friends with most of the guys and they included me."

"What did you do before you were a Boot Knocker?" Her shoulder brushed his.

"Pitched hay, dug fence posts, shoveled manure." They shared a grin and stopped walking.

She turned to him. "From what I hear, you still do those things."

"Yes, but as a Boot Knocker, I have a chance at you."

When she spoke, she was a little breathless. "I don't know what made me ask for you to join us."

He wrapped his fingers around her wrists and slid them upward, to elbows then upper arms. Her eyes were deep pools he could drown in. "It was a damn good decision, Lissy."

"I like the way you drawl my name."

Leaning close, he let his breath tease her ear. "I like the way you taste."

A shiver rippled through her, and he eased closer until she was pressed flush against him. Soft breasts, toned body. His cock ached.

He took her mouth. Passion flared bright and hot, but he kept the kiss controlled, guiding his tongue along hers. Crushing her to his chest and losing himself in the thudding of his pulse.

One of the horses nickered, and Lissy reached up to thread her fingers into Paul's hair. Growling, he pulled away before he scared her by grinding his erection into her.

He took her hand again. "Let's ride. I wanted to show you something."

They picked their way along a valley for about half an hour, throwing each other little glances all the way. When the cabin loomed into view, she stopped.

"What is it?"

"Old trapper's cabin. The man who owned this land had about a thousand acres back in the day. He would run for weeks at a time, checking traps. Of course now the land's been sold off. The Boot Knockers own some, and some went to neighboring ranches."

"But the structure looks sound, not old at all."

She plodded closer, and Paul came up beside her. "That's because I spent some time upkeeping it."

Her gaze flashed to his. "Did you live here?"

"Stayed here plenty of nights. That was before I was a Boot Knocker, though. Now I hang around the ranch."

Her face was alive with excitement. "Can we go inside?"

"Sure, as long as you're not afraid of spiders. It's been a while since I've given it an airing."

She made a dismissive noise and swung off her horse. Paul followed and reached around her to open the door. The wood was a bit swollen and he had to force it.

"No locks?" she asked.

"There's nothing to steal, and if someone needed shelter for the night, he's welcome to it."

"I like that philosophy." She entered before him, looking around at the dim space. The single window didn't allow much light to enter, especially since it was so small and the log walls were dark. It smelled musty but the breeze rushing into the space was quickly helping.

She stood in the center, and Paul came up behind her. Sliding his arms around her and nuzzling her neck felt as right as a rainbow after a hard rain.

She relaxed against him, though he felt a tension in her muscles. Did she want more? Not yet. If he was going to have her, it would be with Jack.

The thought was an odd one, but he had to go with his gut instinct on this. When she wiggled closer, pressing her lush ass against his groin, he almost lost his precarious grip on control.

"Keep moving like that, baby, and I won't be able to keep from taking you."

"Mmm." She shifted again, and he bit off a growl.

"I mean it, Lissy."

"I'm not against it."

He stilled, heart pounding. He wanted her — bad. Jack realized this might happen and he'd technically had no exclusive rights to Lissy. Yet Paul couldn't get the man's flavor out of his head, especially when he'd kissed him last time and found Lissy's taste mingled with Jack's.

"Jack will be waiting for us."

She turned into his arms and slid her arms around his shoulders. "I want that."

He didn't respond, and she studied his eyes.

"Jack told me you haven't been with him before."

"No." He swallowed hard against the sudden surge of lust.

"Well, I'd never been with a man completely until Jack. Itwas the best moment of my life."

Was she suggesting Paul would feel the same?

A breath whooshed from him, and he tipped his forehead against hers. The ache inside him wasn't only for Lissy, and he needed to do something about it. She'd been brave enough to come to the ranch and then to ask for more than one cowboy. Paul had to find the same courage.

More and more over the past few days he'd been able to picture himself in a brand-new way with Jack. As lovers. He could do it—wanted it.

"Let's go down to the ranch and find Jack." His voice came out gruffer than intended.

Lissy's smile was as radiant as the sun he'd once believed burned only for Texas. "Let's do that."

* * * * *

Once Lissy and Paul made it back to the barn, she was ready for more of this adventure — her panties were wet and her mind whirled with lurid visions of how Paul would be in bed.

With Jack.

"I'm going to find Jack. Will you come with me?" Paul's lips were entirely too distracting for her liking. They made her think of long summer nights together, then cooler winter ones.

"I think I'll stay here if you don't mind. The view is incredible."

He touched her arm, and electricity sizzled up to her shoulder. "Okay, I'll be right back with him."

She watched him lope through the field toward the valley. For long minutes, she waited, but sitting still had her on the verge of ripping out her hair. She had to get out of here.

In a rush she made a decision. She hurriedly unsaddled her horse and headed right to a stall housing a fifteen-hand Appaloosa.

It was thick and wouldn't be as agile for high jumps, but it wouldn't balk from scary jumps. And Lissy felt a little reckless.

She quickly outfitted it with bit, bridle and saddle. By the time she swung onto its back, she was edgier than ever.

Why had she even asked for a threesome? Before coming to the ranch, the idea had never surfaced. Why now?

It was the yearning she'd seen in Jack when he'd looked at the other cowboy. If she was honest, she wanted to see him in action with a man like Paul. Then she'd stepped onto the football field with him and gone a little crazy over his rugged good looks.

Her gut instinct had been to request the threesome, and it was too late to take it back.

She rode.

The wind's fingers trailed through her hair, lifting the hot strands from her scalp. A tendril caught in the corner of her mouth and she shook her head to free it. Leaning over her mount, she kicked it into a gallop.

They cut across the ranch, headed straight for a row of fence. The first jump was easy. She wheeled the horse around and nudged him toward a series of gates that could be opened into several configurations to isolate certain animals.

She jumped and jumped again. Sailing over the fence, she got a feel for the horse she'd hijacked. The animal was sturdy and eager to do her bidding. When it tried to hesitate, she pulled back a bit, and he responded beautifully.

Another series of jumps and she grew aware of eyes on her.

Turning her head, she found two strong, tall figures side by side at the outer fence. With a jolt, she realized it was Jack and Paul.

Waiting for her.

Her heart kicked into a brand-new rhythm. A little erratic but a lot erotic. Warmth spread through her lower belly.

She sent the horse careening around the outer ring of fencing. The guys followed her movement. Showing off a little, she completed a double jump that would have won her a blue ribbon.

Really, she was stalling. As soon as she completed this little feat of skills, she'd have no choice but to walk up to the men.

Paul's hat was tipped oh, so low. The way he and Jack leaned slightly toward each other made Lissy's nipples pebble. Having two incredibly hot cowboys might kill her.

Her breath rushed from her as the horse hit the ground running. Now that the animal had gotten a taste for jumping, he wasn't ready to stop. She gave him his head and allowed him to execute a few more jumps before reining him in.

She walked him for a long time, around and around the outer circle, letting him cool down.

When she could stall no more, she trotted over to the guys.

Jack's grin split her heart. Total happiness flooded out. He reached for the reins, and she gave them up. He clicked to her horse, and it stopped. Paul came around the side, reaching up for her.

Lissy looked into his ice-blue eyes. Electricity snapped between them, and that heat in her belly fanned into a wildfire. She tipped into his arms.

"Hey, baby," he drawled.

God, why was she shaking? Paul set her on her feet but didn't release her. His hold on her waist was gentle yet purposeful. He let his gaze roam over her for several seconds.

She noted the creases at the corners of his eyes and the little scar on his upper lip where the hair didn't grow. His lips were wide and kissable, making her think of those long nights again. She felt caught in his web, unable to see much outside of his ensnaring gaze.

Jack took the horse away, obviously giving her a few minutes alone with Paul.

Paul eyed her as if prepared to tell her something big. *Please don't let him back out of the threesome.*

When he spoke, his tone was rough. "I think you should know I took your file from the office. The one with all your personal information that the Boot Knockers don't have access to."

Stunned, she asked, "Why?"

"I had to see more of you. If I'd been able to fight for you, I would have."

"Does Jack know?"

"No."

So he'd wanted her from the beginning too. The knowledge sent a spear of want directly to her pussy. It clenched.

Paul traced light circles on her palms with his thumbs, sending spikes of need through her.

He smelled clean, like soap and grass. During their ride earlier he'd rolled his shirtsleeves to the elbows, the pearl buttons glinting in the sun. His jeans rode low on his hips, worn at the knees. He filled out his clothes very well, and she'd loved the way he felt. She had no reason to be nervous now. She'd had his tongue in her mouth several times.

"Like what you see?" Amusement tinged his low voice.

She nudged him. "You know I do."

Jack returned and walked right up to them. He invaded their space, taking control in a way Lissy had hoped for. She was out of her element here, but Jack would guide her. She had a feeling Paul would know exactly what to do once they started.

Bracing his arms on the fence, one beside Lissy and one beside Paul, he trapped them both with his body. Paul was flush against her, his gaze intense.

"The horse is rubbed down. Do you want to go back to the bungalow?" His breath washed over Lissy's cheek.

She met his gaze and nodded.

As one the three of them turned. Jack pinned a hand to her spine while Paul grabbed her hand. The walk from the barn seemed endless, and she cast about for something to say. In the end, she couldn't think of anything, but that might be best.

Jack led her up the steps of the bungalow. Having Paul at her back made her skin tingle, and when he closed the door behind them all, her heart tripped.

The guys' gazes clashed. "I'll let you lead," Jack said quietly.

Paul nodded.

Lissy could barely hold still.

"Should we have some drinks?" Paul asked. He crossed the main living space to a small bar in the corner. The mini fridge held beer, water and soda. But he grabbed a bottle of whiskey and sloshed it into three shot glasses.

Yes, maybe they all needed a little liquid courage. She accepted the glass from him, as did Jack. They stood in a ring.

"To new horizons," Jack said, lifting his glass.

He shot the whiskey back with a flick of his wrist. Paul's eyes burned into Lissy's as he raised the glass to his lips. She watched the amber liquid disappear into his mouth, then traced the movement of his throat.

She set her glass down and bent to retrieve a bottle of water from the fridge. She twisted off the cap and filled her mouth with cold heaven. After her ride—and with the presence of two stud cowboys—she was parched.

Jack removed the bottle from her hand. When he curled his fingers around her nape and drew her in for a kiss, she quivered.

The first hot lash of his whiskey-flavored tongue sent her reeling. She gasped, and he took advantage of her open mouth. He kissed her long and deep, cradling her head and her ass in two big hands.

When he broke away, Paul swooped in. Without hesitation, he took control. His taste was so different yet so good. Whiskey, man and need.

Dark lust heated her core.

Paul wrapped her in his arms, holding her tight enough that she felt every rigid inch of his body — *every* inch.

For long minutes he explored her, snaking his tongue over her lips, teeth, tongue. Then touching her hair, shoulders, back, right down to cup her ass. His grip made her suck in a gasp.

Jack inched near, nuzzling her throat while Paul ran his hands up to squeeze her breasts.

Her skin erupted in gooseflesh, and her pussy grew slick.

They raised their heads and an unspoken agreement passed between them. In a flash Lissy found herself in the bedroom. The bed had been made with fresh sheets while she was out, and it seemed a shame to rumple the perfection.

Jack didn't think so, however. He laid her down and covered her with his body. Paul sank to the bed's edge. Rearing up onto his knees, Jack faced the cowboy.

"Let me." He slowly removed Paul's hat, revealing short blond hair streaked with brown.

Paul sank his teeth into his lower lip, and Lissy sat up, unable to tear her gaze away from the pair. The air crackled with excitement and attraction. Breathless, she leaned on her elbows.

Jack tipped his head so close to Paul's. The man's chest heaved, but he didn't move away. The anticipation on Jack's handsome features was one of the most beautiful things she'd ever witnessed.

"It's time," Paul grated out.

When hard lips brushed hard lips, she couldn't contain the noise that escaped her.

* * * * *

Paul was going to die of need. At last, he had Jack's mouth under his, and while the man had kissed him plenty of times, Paul hadn't been ready then. With excruciating slowness, he moved his lips. Jack's breath rushed out. Emotion mounted in Paul's chest as he angled his head and tasted him more fully. Jack moved in just the right ways while giving Paul the upper hand.

Paul opened his eyes and stared into his friend's. Up close they held traces of burning need that was probably reflected in his own eyes.

A quiet groan vibrating in his chest, Paul framed Jack's face with his hands and kissed him harder. Jack grunted, and Paul couldn't stop himself. He plunged his tongue between his best friend's lips.

Need twisted in his gut. His balls ached, and his cock was an iron staff behind his zipper. Their kisses before were tame compared to this. He drank deeply from his friend — soon to be lover. As he gathered the flavors into his head, his thoughts shifted into place.

He was almost ready.

The kiss raged out of control. Tongues seeking, chasing, exploring. Paul slammed his mouth over Jack's, almost bruising and so good. They locked their arms around each other and Paul wrestled him to the mattress.

Jack's submission eased Paul into the new territory. Right now he didn't need Jack's aggression. He needed to do this his way.

Lissy released a quiet mewl of desire, and they tore away from each other. Panting hard, Paul climbed off Jack. They turned to Lissy.

"Fuck, you look delicious, baby. Get her top off, Paul. I'll take the bottoms."

She squirmed, her hair fanning out on the light blue bedding. Paul kissed her long and lingeringly, tangling tongues with more emotion than he'd ever expected.

She threw herself into the kiss, and in seconds passion raged. She raked her fingers over his shirt buttons as he twisted her tank top under his fingers. They stripped each other. Paul fumbled over her bra clasp even as she fought his buttons. But in the end, they both won.

They'd all win.

Jack yanked his shirt overhead and abandoned it on the plush carpet. He reached for Lissy's waistband while small squeaks left her throat, and Paul captured them. He fed a long groan back into her mouth.

Boots all hit the floor. Jack shimmied her jeans down her lean hips and off her legs. The long line of muscle flexed as he walked his fingers back up to catch her panties. With a violent tug, he stripped her.

Juices glistened on her folds, and the scent of her arousal struck him hard.

"Fuck, she smells good," Paul rasped. And she looked like heaven. Perfectly curved, strong and lithe. She'd fit perfectly against him — and Jack.

Lissy reached for Paul's belt buckle, but he rocked his hips out of reach. "Baby, I can't last if you touch me right now. First I'm going to make you scream."

She cooed, eyes the color of midnight. Paul bundled her hair off her neck and laved a path up to her delicate jaw. When Paul looked up into his best friend's eyes, his heart beat heavier. This felt right and he wanted it. They'd built up long enough.

Leaning in, Jack trapped her plump nipple between his lips and plucked it. Paul moved in and took the other. When Jack lifted his head, Paul couldn't resist pulling him into a kiss.

He tasted of Lissy. Grunting, Paul sank his tongue into Jack's mouth over and over while Lissy wriggled restlessly beneath them.

As they tore free of each other, Jack guided Paul down her body. "You get the first taste."

Lissy moaned.

With a grin, Paul positioned himself between her thighs. He spread them and wrapped them around his ears. Then with one open-mouthed bite, he made her scream.

She threw her head back, neck cords straining. Jack claimed her mouth, swallowing her sounds as Paul worked her clit with swift revolutions of his tongue. Taking her nipple between his teeth, Jack lightly tugged. Paul closed his eyes and lapped her wet folds until Lissy began to shake. They teased and tormented her. The bed quaked.

Then Paul thrust a big finger deep into her center, and she came apart. He sucked on her clit and finger-fucked her while Jack stole another kiss.

As her final convulsions fled, Paul surged upward.

"Gimme a taste," Jack said.

They came together with a primal crash. Paul's lips were coated in her juices. Unable to stop himself, Paul reached for his lover's jeans. A snap of his wrist and the button popped. Heart pounding, he eased down the zipper and reached in, pulling Jack's cock free.

It slid into his hand, thick and veined. As Paul learned every contour, he watched Jack's face contort in pleasure. Maybe he'd found something he was really good at.

Paul jacked him slowly, from base to tip. The head was plump and the cap purple with need. Lissy regained her senses, and together they pushed Jack down on the mattress. His eyes were wide and glazed, but he didn't make a move.

Lissy speckled Jack's neck and chest with kisses, taking her time to bite his perfect nipples with those scorching hot gold hoops. Paul divested him of his jeans and underwear.

He scrubbed a hand over his face. Fuck, he was going to explode just from watching the bliss on Jack's features.

He smelled of man and musk. How would he taste? At the idea of backing off, Paul's stomach plummeted. No, he wanted this. If he were honest with himself, he'd been growing closer to this moment each day. Jack had become more than his best friend.

He licked his lips and Jack caught him. The dark look they exchanged drew Paul closer.

The trim lines of Jack's legs led right up to a shadowed area. Paul's balls ached and he wet his lips again.

Seeing Paul's hesitation, Jack said, "Why don't we change places? You don't have to do this, man."

Paul shook his head. "No. Just—I want this." That shadowed spot tormented the hell out of him, and like a kid told not to go exploring, Paul's instinct was to do the exactly opposite. Swallowing hard, Paul let his gaze tick over Jack once again. Something was building inside him—something huge. He didn't just want this—he needed it. All those kisses he'd pushed away from, and those that he hadn't, fed into a sharp realization about who he really was.

He wasn't going to deny his attraction to Jack anymore. And he wasn't going to deny himself the satisfaction he knew he'd get from the man in return.

Slowly he wrapped his fingers around Jack's length. Jack went completely still, watching through hooded eyes. Seeing the effect he had on his friend, he gave a test stroke.

Jack groaned, eyes rolling up his head.

Feeling more powerful, Paul slid Jack's erection through his palm. Eliciting another groan, he continued to fist his cock. A bead of pre-come pooled in the depression.

He could stop and trade places, letting Jack blow his mind by sucking his cock. It seemed a natural progression since Paul was the inexperienced one. But he'd never backed down from a challenge, and right now, keeping Jack speechless was the ultimate goal.

Jack's hips lifted as Paul ran his thick head through his fist. Their gazes met. What Paul saw there spurred him on. Before he could think too hard about his decision, he sprawled on the bed and swallowed Jack's cock.

Jack bucked into his mouth. "Fuck," he bit off.

Lissy lapped a circle around Jack's nipple while Paul savored the fullness in his mouth. Passion flared, and his own cock distended even more. Hell, he wasn't going to last.

He traced a path up the hard shaft to the leaking tip. When he gathered the cream there, all three of them moaned.

Jack grabbed the back of Paul's head and pushed him all the way down. It hit the back of his throat, and he swallowed. Jack's thigh muscles locked, his abs tightened. He fucked his cock deep into Paul's mouth, and he took it right to the base.

"Fucking hell," Jack ground out a split second before a thick jet of come filled Paul's mouth.

He swallowed the sweet essence. He had no idea why he'd waited so long for this moment.

* * * * *

Jack succumbed to the best blowjob of his life. Every pull of Paul's mouth drew more and more from him. Lissy's soft hair trailed over his body while nipping his skin. He shuddered as the last of his orgasm filled Paul's mouth.

Paul eased the pressure of his mouth, taking him more gently. Lissy fell back on the bed, tanned limbs stretched out and her eyes vibrant blue. She parted her thighs and strummed her clit with two fingers.

A throaty noise left Jack. Holding her gaze, he regained his senses as Lissy's fingers grew wet with her juices.

He clasped a hand around Paul's jaw and slipped free of his lover's mouth. Paul's gaze burned into him, scorching in a way he'd never get over if he lived to be a hundred.

"It was time," Paul repeated. They shared a smile that was part playful, part emotion. Jack had seen that burning in Paul's eyes before he'd kissed him in the bunkhouse, then again at the fence. Yet now it was amplified. Paul scuffed his rough stubble over Jack's inner thigh, making him suck in a sharp breath.

Paul rumbled a laugh, obviously getting off on how he affected Jack.

Lissy hummed in pleasure as she dashed her fingers over her swollen bud. Paul and Jack exchanged a look. Just as they banded together on a ranch chore, they were united in this bedroom.

Paul climbed off the mattress and stood at the side of the bed, cock in hand, as if unsure what to do next.

"Time to return the favor," Jack said, urging Paul forward. Jack was in a perfect position to take him into his mouth, and hell, he'd been dying to for a long time.

Paul's throat worked as he swallowed. For a heart-stopping moment Jack feared he'd say no, he wasn't going to let him touch him.

Dark want slithered through Paul's eyes. His erection twitched. Paul gave a slight nod, and Jack didn't hesitate. He clutched Paul's hard ass and dragged him into his mouth. By the time the fat head filled the back of his throat, Jack was completely hard again.

Paul threw his head back and released a guttural groan. Lissy cried out, gaze riveted on them.

"Hell, Jack. I never knew—"

Jack hummed in answer, lapping a swath up the side of his fat cock. Jesus, he'd hungered for this moment forever. Really, it was the look in his lover's eyes that made the experience complete, though.

Eyes lidded, Paul grated out, "Put a condom on him and straddle him, baby."

The mattress shook as Lissy climbed off the bed. A second later her nimble fingers were working a rubber over Jack's dick. Spikes of want speared him. He sucked on Paul's cock, hoping to deliver the same pleasure as he'd given him.

Running his tongue around the underside of the head, he looked up to catch Lissy's stare. She settled her thighs around him, her tight, hot pussy poised at the tip of his erection.

Paul groaned, his cock jerking in Jack's mouth. Planting a hand on his lover's ass, Jack dragged him deeper even as Lissy sank onto him.

Jack lost himself to sensation. Her walls clamping around him, Paul filling his mouth. Jack's tanned fingers closed around Lissy's pink nipples. The bed rocked as the three of them found a rhythm.

Suddenly Paul pulled his cock free. A smile played around his lips as he stared down at Jack. "As much as I want to unload in your mouth, I want to give Lissy more pleasure than she's ever had."

Hell. Jack tried not to show his disappointment as Paul pulled Lissy off him. But when he eased her up so her wet pussy hovered over Jack's face, he couldn't resist a rumble of pleasure.

Paul fiddled with his own condom. Then he lashed an arm around her middle and sank his cock into her core. She cried out, and Jack licked her clit. Just as they got into a rhythm, Paul's fist captured Jack's shaft again.

The three of them moved in unison, Lissy's body the center of it all. Her hair bounced on her shoulders and her breasts bounced The dark pressure building in Jack's groin was too close to the surface.

Lissy's bud hardened under Jack's tongue. He flattened it. Hips jerking, Paul thrust into her. Her body rolled between them, and Paul's fist was so damn good —

She came first with a rough cry. As Jack guided her along the rocky cliff of ecstasy, his balls throbbed. The spot at the base of his spine tingled. In a rush, he came again. Hot spurts filled the condom he wore.

Suddenly Paul was bucking hard and fast, his mouth opened on an O of pleasure.

They continued to move, their motions growing slower. When Lissy slid boneless to the mattress, Paul tucked her against his side while Jack plastered her back with his body. Their breathing slowed and sweat dried.

When Jack opened his eyes, Lissy was staring at him, eyes glassy and her lips ripe.

Those hours they'd spent in this very bed seemed like foreplay compared to this session.

Jack tentatively reached across Lissy and stroked a finger over Paul's square jaw. Their gazes locked.

"We okay, man?" he asked.

"Actually, there's something I have to tell you." Paul's eyes were serious, his mouth unsmiling.

Jack's heart clenched and he was barely able to force out the words. "What's that?"

Lissy looked between them.

Paul placed a hand on her flat belly as he leaned over to stare into Jack's eyes. "I don't know why I waited. You suck cock better than anyone I've ever known in my life."

Jack barked a laugh just as Lissy surged upward, throwing out her arms. "Wait. You can't make that decision yet. You haven't given me a chance to compete."

Chapter Seven

Steam rose from the water and wove around Jack as he sank into the hot tub. Pleasure crossed his face, but Lissy didn't notice that too long. She was too busy being jealous of the dew on his chest. She wanted to be those water droplets.

His muscles rippled as he took a seat in the water. Paul rounded the corner, and her breath caught. Damn, he looked good in a towel. His chiseled abs drew her attention — until he dropped the terrycloth.

He stepped into the water and extended a hand to her. "Come in, darlin'."

Fighting the shiver that raced down her spine, she took his hand and dipped a toe into the hot water. Groaning, she stepped in all the way and seated herself next to Jack. Paul pressed close on her other side.

The jets spewed bubbles, and she focused on them until her vision blurred. How had she gotten here? Not only to the ranch but how had she become a cowboy sandwich filling?

Muscles hemmed her in. They'd just blown her mind, and it seemed Paul had broken through the barrier that had once held him back. He relaxed against the back of the hot tub, arms stretched out and his hand on Jack's shoulder. Their camaraderie was evident, but the way they stared at each other… Lissy had a hard time looking away.

"Lean back," Jack said, his hand heavy on her upper thigh. She rested her head against his shoulder and snuggled against Paul's side.

Fatigue washed through her as the heat and jets massaged her. The hot tub was set between high walls, hidden from the ranch. The guys had assured her the others were in the auditorium and no one would see them.

"What's going on in the auditorium?" she asked.

"A munch," Jack said.

She flushed to the roots of her hair, imagining all those cowboys taking turns "munching" on the women.

"It's a term for a social gathering for people interested in BDSM. We have one most weeks."

"Oh."

"We didn't think you'd want to, but if you wanna go —"

She cut Jack off. "No. I'm happy with the hot tub."

Damn, was she. Best decision ever.

Smiling to herself, she felt her muscles loosen a little more.

Paul's fingers came at her, walking up until Jack's joined his and eight fingers met at the V of her legs. How was it possible that she was instantly revving already? She'd just had two huge orgasms and countless ones with Jack in the days leading up to this.

Paul spread her pussy lips, and Jack delved his finger inside.

"Ahhhh." She squeezed her eyes closed, letting them take over. They pressed her between them, and she heard the wet meeting of lips. Jack teased her inner walls with slow finger thrusts, curling the tip against a spot that made her pussy flood.

The hot tub sputtered and the bubbles stopped. With a grunt, Paul removed his hand. Lissy bit off a moan of disappointment.

"Damn jets." Paul got out of the hot tub, water streaming off his tanned flesh and cutting paths through his thigh hair. She and Jack watched him circle around the unit that obviously housed the controls.

He dried his hands on a towel and slung it over his shoulder. Seeing a man crouch in the buff was...whoooeee. Lissy would have started sweating if she wasn't already so warm.

"Nice fucking view, man," Jack said.

Paul shot him a grin before opening the panel and fiddling around. A second later the jets hummed to life again, and bubbles popped around them.

As Paul strutted back to their seat, she could see how proud he was of himself.

"Paul's Mr. Fix-It around here. Even though he spends his days in the bungalows, he's often called out to repair things on the ranch."

"I don't mind. I enjoy working with my hands."

Jack arched a long brow. "Is that so?" With that, he grabbed Paul's hand and yanked it across Lissy to cover his cock.

The intense expression in Paul's eyes said he was bone-deep into this arrangement. Lissy was deeper, though. She felt right at home here—under the Texas sky, on the ranch, in the arms of Jack and now Paul.

Leaning in slowly, Paul kissed her while groping Jack. She accepted his tongue, tasting

246

and swirling hers against his. Jack buried his fingers in her again, and she gasped at the thickness.

He had to have three fingers inside her. Walls stretching, she gave herself up to them. Paul kissed her while Jack sucked a nipple and fingered her. A low burn took over her belly.

As if they'd choreographed it, both men pulled away. Paul reached over the side and grabbed two condoms from a little pile she hadn't noticed before. When they stood, water sluiced off their hard forms. Their erections jutted at her, and her mouth watered.

Paul had his on first. He gripped her upper arms and whirled her, pinning her to the side. In one slow thrust, he filled her. She thought she'd go a little crazy, but his hot whispers ripped away her control entirely.

"Fuck, baby, you're so hot. So tight." He circled his hips, reaching deep. She cried out and dropped her head back against his shoulder. He dotted her skin with kisses, his erotic words coming faster. "I wanted you so damn bad. I hated Jack for having you."

* * * * *

"Hey, I shared." Jack wrapped his arms around Paul from behind, his erection pressed firmly against Paul's ass.

Paul had only had one other person touch his ass in his lifetime—an adventurous girl in his early twenties before he'd become a Boot Knocker. She'd lubed a finger and toyed with his backside for what felt like hours. It wasn't until he was balls-deep inside her that he realized her finger was gliding over his prostate.

The sensation of Jack's cock against his taboo spot ricocheted through him. Nerve endings more alive than ever, he tried to center himself. Did he want this? Jack's cock inside him?

Not yet.

He grasped Jack's hip and tried to slow his movements.

But Jack didn't attempt to enter him. He only rocked against him, drawing the swollen head of his cock over Paul's pucker until he thought he'd lose it.

Need engulfing him, he ground out, "I'm going to make you come so hard you forget your name."

She writhed, trying to bring him deeper. He clutched her hips under the water and yanked her against him hard. Again and again. Her breathing grew choppier and his movements more erratic. His cock speared her high, and the first contraction gripped him.

He groaned.

Jack sealed himself against Paul, sliding his cock along Paul's ass.

Lissy panted as Paul fucked her and Jack mimicked fucking him. Maybe Paul wasn't ready, but two days ago he never would have gone this far. And touching Jack didn't seem odd anymore. He couldn't imagine having any other man this way, though.

Lissy shattered around him, and he couldn't still his movements.

When Jack eased a finger into his ass, he ground his teeth against the over-the-top feelings. Lissy clenching and releasing around him, Jack's finger expanding him...

While Lissy still pulsated and jerked in his hold, he pulled free of her body, grabbed Jack and laid one on him.

The hard crush of lips raised a guttural growl from his throat. He pushed Jack forward so he sank into Lissy's freshly fucked pussy.

And then Paul entered his best friend in slow increments.

The feelings Jack had roused in him more and more every time he pursued Paul narrowed to one pinpoint of emotion — he wanted this. His best friend kissed like a pro and sucked cock even better. He'd feel amazing wrapped around Paul's cock. While he wasn't ready to be on the receiving end, he loved that Jack was willing to give up control.

That he trusted Paul enough.

Paul loved so many things about Jack. His scent, his laugh, his damn soft-eyed looks. Throat constricting, he slid in a fraction at a time, letting his lover grow accustomed to him. But he'd heard that Jack bottomed a lot, and he took him easily.

Every damn, tooth-grinding inch.

He hissed as his balls swung against Jack's hard ass. Out of control, he began to move. Sinking into him over and over and propelling Jack into Lissy. Her moans were sweet music.

"Goddamn. Jack—" He broke off as need escalated. He was so close, but he wanted Jack there with him. He reached around Jack's hard torso and found those golden hoops in his nipples that he could now admit distracted the hell out of him.

"Yesss," Jack bowed back, taking every inch as he simultaneously thrust into Lissy.

Her noises increased. Jack's body clamped around Paul's cock, and he couldn't hold back the roar.

His orgasm stole all thought. White haze, soft cries, a grunt of release and the burble of water. The several seconds it took to empty his balls felt much longer.

Jack hunched forward, kissing Lissy's nape. Emotion wrapped around Paul's heart, tugging strings he hadn't realized he owned.

When he came back to himself, exhaustion made his eyelids droop. He leaned over Jack and bit into the side of his neck.

Jack twisted his head, and Paul grazed his lips with a kiss.

His chest burned as he reluctantly withdrew from Jack's body. Lissy sagged in Jack's hold, and he turned her into his arms to carry her out of the hot tub. Paul helped him dry her, and then they supported her for the walk back to Bungalow 15.

* * * * *

Lissy lay face down on the bed, deliciously sore in all the right places. Over the past few hours she'd used muscles she hadn't known she'd possessed.

Paul's thigh anchored her to the mattress, and Jack's strong arm lay across her upper back. After all those amazing orgasms, she was exhausted. But her mind worked overtime.

"You were poetry on that horse. I never saw jumps like that before," Paul said.

She thought Jack was dozing, but when Paul spoke, he opened his eyes. She smiled and turned her head in Paul's direction. His lips were soft and his expression more open since he'd joined them in the bungalow—and then the hot tub.

Paul stroked her cheek with his knuckles. The gesture grabbed her heart and squeezed. Damn, first Jack and now this. She had to detach herself somehow. They weren't her cowboys. In a few days she'd leave them behind and set off into the world as a changed woman. With any luck she'd find a cowboy of her own, but...

She'd never forget these moments.

"No wonder you've won all those competitions."

"I love to jump."

"What else do you love? Beach volleyball?"

"You really did read my file."

Jack stirred behind her. "What's this about a file?" His voice was groggy.

"Nothing." Paul gave her a conspiratorial wink, which she felt to the soles of her feet. He was a sexy man through and through.

"I do love beach volleyball. It's easy to get caught up."

"Wow. That was a story I just saw cross your face. What's going on in your head?" Paul asked.

Jack gripped her hip and rolled her so he could peer into her face. She caressed his jaw, loving the prickly lines.

She drew a deep breath. "I was thinking how much I love Texas and could easily live here, but there's no beach volleyball. However, I think there are things about Texas that beat the sport I love."

"Like horses and lots of land for riding," Jack said.

And cowboys. Two of them, actually.

"I don't know if I could pick up and move. My friends are too important to me." Jack sent Paul a sidelong look.

"Me too," Paul added, a strange note in his voice. "You're all I've got."

"Bullshit." Jack's smile faded as he saw how serious Paul was.

"All the Boot Knockers are my friends, but you're more like..." His brow crinkled as he struggled to find the right word.

Lissy looked to Jack, who blurted, "Family."

"Yes," Paul said immediately. "With my family holding that grudge against me, I've come to rely on you a lot, Jack."

Jack's eyes shone as he stared at their lover. "You know I just needed your part of the money for the herd. That's the only reason I—" He shook with laughter as Paul steamrolled Lissy and started pummeling him.

He took a light punch to the abs and brought his knee up. Paul blocked him just in time.

Lissy's breath came faster as she watched their antics. "I thought the football in the underwear thing was hot. Naked male wrestling is…oh my God."

Jack hooked her around the neck and dragged her into their clutches. "You're as athletic as we are. I bet you can hold your own in this match."

"Is that a challenge?" She grinned and threw her leg over Paul, locking them both to the bed.

"Oh yes." They grappled for a while before she gave up and let fatigue settle over her limbs again.

Paul spooned her and she plastered herself to Jack's side. She could get used to this. If she wasn't careful, she'd be in deep trouble.

* * * * *

Lissy perched on the fence, watching Paul and Jack work. As they moved through the herd, checking their animals, a tight feeling rooted in her chest. Not only were they beautiful men, they were good men.

Paul had shucked his shirt, and his back muscles rippled as he wrapped his arms around a calf and hefted it off its feet. Jack hurried ahead of him, parting the herd so Paul could pass.

Lissy jumped off the fence and wiped the seat of her jeans. "What's going on?"

"This calf was hurt earlier. We thought it had cleared up, and the vet gave us leave to place it with the rest of the cows, but it's favoring this leg again," Jack explained, his tone gruff. Lissy didn't take it personally — he obviously cared about this animal.

She hurried along the fence and pushed the bolt holding the gate in place. It swung open. Paul passed through, and Jack waved her out too. He closed the gate behind them.

When Paul placed the calf on his horse, an invisible lasso tightened around Lissy's heart. He swung into the saddle behind the animal.

"Wait." Jack clamped a hand on his lover's thigh. Lissy's heart tripped faster as the guys exchanged a look overflowing with meaning.

Paul nodded. His gaze brushed Lissy, and she felt it like the softest caress.

"We'll finish up here and meet you at the barn." Jack moved to Lissy and wrapped an arm around her waist. She leaned against him, watching as Paul trotted down the slope. When he dropped out of sight, Jack turned to her.

His lips were set into a line she immediately recognized as worry.

Brushing a thumb across his lower lip, she asked, "Will you call the vet?"

"Yeah, but I thought you might examine the calf first."

Her shoulders straightened. "Me? I'm a horse specialist. I don't know enough about cows."

"A hurt leg is a hurt leg, right? We'll call the vet, but it can sometimes take him half a day to get here. I'd just like you to look at it." His blue-green eyes would have swayed her even if worry hadn't burned there.

"Of course. I'll take a look."

"Good. Let's finish up chores first."

Stunned, she let Jack lead her into the midst of the animals. His confidence in her shook her world. First he trusted her with the calf and now he was drawing her into their enterprise. It was only checking the animals and filling water troughs, but still, it felt good.

As he slapped a particularly ornery cow in the rump to propel it out of his way, she studied his profile. God, she was falling for him.

Had fallen.

If she didn't have to leave the ranch, she'd want to get to know him better. Paul too. The pair was entangled in her mind.

She'd gotten a two-for-one deal.

Pushing out a sigh, she shook off the fantasy of remaining here and helping them like this every day. Working together, connecting. Suddenly she wanted much more than earth-shattering orgasms.

Jack stepped in front of her, jolting her from her musings. Ducking his head, he slammed a kiss across her lips. Scents of leather and working man filled her head, and she groaned. Before he moved away, she deepened the kiss.

Gliding her tongue along his lip, she urged him to play with her. He didn't disappoint.

Gloved hands locked on her spine as he yanked her close. He slanted his mouth over hers, delving his tongue deep. Dizzy with desire, she threw herself into the kiss. Lust dampened her panties and made her nipples ache. But the emotions swirling like a Texas twister through her were much more powerful.

Soft sounds left her. While she knew it was her body pleading for more, it was her way of telling Jack how strongly she was beginning to feel for him without using words.

She could never tell him. He'd probably dealt with lovesick women before, and she wouldn't become another.

He pinned her to the fence and kissed her until her bones turned to rubber. When he lifted her leg and wrapped it around his hip, she groaned.

His kiss grew savage. Was it her or was the world turning faster? The heavens had united with the earth and meteors rained down around them.

Jack lifted his head, his expression fierce. "I'd take you right here if I didn't think Paul would get pissed at me."

She giggled, utter joy seizing her. She explored Jack's hard biceps bulging the sleeves of his Boot Knockers Ranch T-shirt. "We'd better head down to the barn and find him then."

She started to slip out of his hold, but he jerked her close. Lifting her onto tiptoe, he pressed his lips to her ear. "When I get you between me and Paul, you're going to find it hard to walk away."

Every cell in her body slowed. Swallowing, she tilted her head to meet his gaze. "What do you mean?"

"I might want to keep—" He cut off and let her fall back to her heels. "I just mean that you're going to be so sore you'll remember who made you that way." He ran his knuckle under his nose and looked away.

"Oh." Disappointment washed through her.

He showed her how to open the valve on the water tank in the back of the pickup and fill the troughs with the hose. The sun beat down on her head, prickling her scalp. When she looked over her shoulder, though, he was staring at her, a strange expression on his rugged features.

She sent him a smile, and he did that chin-nod thing that sent streamers of heat straight to her pussy.

I'll take what I can from this week and walk away with amazing memories.

With her resolve firmed once again, she and Jack finished the chores. The bumpy ride down the ridge to the valley seemed to take forever. She was hyperaware of his muscled thighs in worn jeans, the dusting of blond hairs on his knuckles and the sidelong looks he kept giving her.

By the time they got out of the truck, she was edgy. And horny as hell.

Paul came to the barn door, irritation like thunder on his brow. "What took ya so long?" He raked his gaze over Lissy as if looking for disheveled clothes.

"We took our time checking out the other cows. It takes time to show Lissy how to do the chores too." Jack stepped up to him.

Lissy's breath came faster. Her cowboys, chest to chest, were a sight to behold. When she thought of Texas in the future, it would be this, not the enormous sky and the land that was like a campfire song.

Paul's shoulders relaxed, and Jack squeezed his lover's hand. "Where'd you put the calf?"

"The empty stall. Lissy's going to look at it and we called the vet, so we've just made the animal comfortable."

"Yeah? Let's see what's going on, Lissy."

They turned together and disappeared into the dim interior. Lissy rushed forward to examine the calf. Its big, brown, wide-spaced eyes and the little whorls of hair covering its ears were endearing. She prodded the tendons for several seconds. Her mind grew engulfed by the possibilities of the calf's injury.

Finally she sat back on her heels and looked up at Jack and Paul.

"Well?" Jack asked.

"I don't believe it's her leg that's hurt."

"What is it then?" Paul's voice was tense.

She rose to her feet. "What do you know about this calf? What kind of birthing did she have?"

They looked at each other. "We don't know."

"I might be making a stretch with this... I'm not a vet."

"Just tell us what you think is wrong," Jack said gently.

She drew a deep breath. "I think she has some gluteal nerve damage. If she had a hard birth and was pulled out, sometimes the pressure on the hind leg causes nerve damage. The result is one leg is weaker and the animal favors it."

"Damn," Paul said.

"The calf loses balance sometimes? Seems wobbly?"

"Yes, that's right." Jack moved so close to Paul their shoulders brushed. The warmth in Lissy's belly coiled.

"What's to be done about it?" Paul asked.

"Only the vet will know for sure, but I believe it's better if she's not lying in the same position for long periods of time. Being on her feet will help."

"Shit. We shouldn't have taken her out of the pasture." Jack crouched and touched the calf's soft ear. It flicked, and they all laughed. Some of the tension dissolved.

"This could possibly resolve on its own. Animals are resilient." Lissy smiled at Paul.

"Maybe we should have gotten horses," he said.

"I'd know for sure if it was a horse instead. But it's my best guess."

Paul cradled her cheek in his big, rough hand. Sparks flowed like an electrical current between their gazes. "Thank you, baby."

She swayed toward him. "Of course. I wish I could do more. And the vet will know for sure."

"Thank you, baby. You deserve a reward." His other hand closed around her breast, eliciting a moan from her.

He rubbed his thumb back and forth over her nipple until it pebbled. Pressure slithered through her core, and she whimpered. Jack's body closed in from behind, gently crushing her between her cowboys.

She couldn't think of anyplace she'd rather be.

Jack lifted her into Paul's arms. She wrapped her legs around his waist, and his erection jutted against her pussy. As he turned to leave the stall with her, Jack slipped out too and closed the door.

"Where are you taking me?" She snuggled close to Paul.

"Bed." His tone was low and deep, the drawl perfect. Shivers ran down her spine. They left the barn and Paul carried her across the lawn to Bungalow 15. Jack opened the door, and they all spilled inside.

The cooler air kissed her skin, raising goose bumps. Paul bit into her earlobe and worried it back and forth. "I'm going to strip you and watch Jack eat your pussy. Then I'm going to take over and make you scream."

Aching at his words, she hummed a response. Paul set her on her feet, and Jack whirled her to face him. His eyes were two candles as he swooped in to claim her mouth. While he kissed the panties off her, Paul kneaded her breasts from behind. And the way he ground his hips into hers...

She ran one hand down Jack's chest and reached behind to touch Paul. She wished she had more hands.

When they bundled her into the bedroom, she was a shaking mess of need. Paul took care of her boots while Jack removed her top. Together, they stripped off her jeans. She stood before them in only panties and a sports bra.

She wasn't often self-conscious. She was proud of her body and what her active lifestyle had created. But right now, with four eyes in two shades of blue on her, she trembled.

"Fucking gorgeous," Jack grated out.

"Stunning. I've gotta have you." Paul reached for her, but Jack was quicker. He tossed Lissy to the bed and prostrated herself between her thighs.

She huffed out a laugh at Paul's expression. "You did say Jack would have first dibs."

Rumbling a laugh, Jack ensnared the side of her panties in his teeth and tugged them down. His heated breath and rough beard ignited her. She waved at Paul to come closer.

As if understanding her desire, he unbuckled his jeans and freed his cock. When the thick tip probed her lips, she moaned and opened to accept him.

Jack opened his mouth over her pussy. She cried out as one filled her and the other tasted her. Juices pooled between her nether lips as she ran her tongue over Paul's rigid cock.

He pushed deeper into her, and she stared into his eyes, noting the glassiness of his. Doubling her efforts, she sucked him into her throat. Jack groaned and lapped a path up and down her folds that made her squirm.

She bucked into his tongue, taking what she needed even as Paul worked his cock in and out of her mouth.

* * * * *

Damn, this beautiful woman was a master with her mouth. With every swipe of her talented tongue he rocketed up the steep slope toward bliss. The wet sounds of Jack licking her pussy filled the air, along with her scents of arousal.

Fucking hot. Gorgeous. He wouldn't forget this woman.

Especially since she'd brought Jack into his life in a brand-new way. Lissy was so special, and they would both miss the hell out of her when she left in a few days.

Emotion snagged his heart, and the hazy-eyed look she gave him set the hook. He cradled her head and lost himself in sensation.

Heat clenched his balls against his body. No, that was Lissy's fingers. He grunted and threw his head back as she teased the underside. When she continued toward his pucker, he spread his legs and gave her access.

The strokes of her tongue and fingers blew his mind. As Jack drove her closer to her pinnacle, tiny sounds escaped her. Christ, Paul wasn't going to last.

He had to last.

Twitching his hips so he was out of reach, he did as he promised and took over Jack's role. When Lissy's flavors coated his lips and tongue, he feared he'd lose control and come all over the bed.

Eyes glittering, Jack fed his cock slowly into Lissy's mouth. Want pooled low in Paul's groin. It was impossible not to knot the feelings of true friendship, camaraderie and affection with the sheer lust he'd felt while pounding into Jack's tight ass.

He circled Lissy's clit. The bud strained under his tongue, and he knew she was so close. She clamped her lips around Jack's shaft and sucked noisily.

"Shhhit," Jack murmured, leg muscles shaking.

Planting his hands on her thighs, Paul thrust his tongue into her soaking channel. Cream, need, beautiful woman he didn't want to let go.

He tongue-fucked her until her hips jerked off the bed. The first pulsation drew a long moan from her, and Jack jerked his cock free of her lips, probably struggling to keep from unloading as well.

Lissy's face flushed pink as her orgasm swept her. Jack pushed two fingers into her mouth, and she sucked as her pussy clenched and released around Paul's tongue.

Jack swung his gaze toward Paul. Their eyes met. In that moment, everything slipped into place like tumblers in a lock. Friends to lovers and in charge of Lissy's pleasure.

As Lissy convulsed with her release, Paul removed his tongue and flipped her over. He jerked her ass toward him and burrowed his tongue deep.

She cried out, fisting the sheets. Paul didn't let up. With one finger he kept her coming while he teased her behind. He had to prepare her because sooner or later he and Jack would take her together. It might not be today, but they would share space in her body before she left the ranch.

He learned every ridge of her rim with his tongue. When he felt her loosen, he eased his finger upward, painting her juices on her ass. The tip slipped inside.

She pushed back, her face pinker. He sank his finger into her millimeter by millimeter. When his finger was buried to the knuckle, he almost lost it.

"Oh God, it feels so good," she whimpered.

"Paul," Jack said in a tight voice. He looked up. Jack's eyes were dark with wanting, and he squeezed his cock so the tip was purple, trying to stave off his orgasm.

Jack was right. Not today. With exquisite slowness, he pulled his finger free. Then he got off the bed. A swig of an old beer left on the nightstand and a condom in place, and he was ready.

While pounding into Jack's body, he'd been desperate to get closer, to stake some claim on him.

The only way he knew how to gain that was to give himself to Jack.

Jack was pulling Lissy up into his arms. Paul's mind took snapshots of the moment. He'd leave this room a changed man. While that scared the hell out of him, it excited him too.

He looked into Jack's eyes. "Get a condom on." He hoped his words were infused with the meaning he intended.

Jack's face transformed with understanding. Pure joy lit his features as he scrambled off the bed. Lissy was in a daze, but not for long. Paul laid her down and covered her with his body.

The kiss they shared was tender and slow. She hooked her thighs around his waist, and he slowly sank into her body. As her inner walls hugged him, he felt Jack's thighs against his from behind.

Lissy made a sound. Jack bit into Paul's neck lightly as he let him get used to the tip of his cock against his opening. He rubbed for several minutes. Paul moved in and out of Lissy's tight sheath, watching emotions play over her face.

Paul heard the sound of a lube cap popping and prepared himself for Jack's touch. He wasn't ready for the amazing sensation of Jack's big fingers spreading lube over his ass. Or the finger he invaded with.

His lover stretched him, working the lube inside, taking his time and making it good for Paul.

Panting, he pressed back, eager for a second finger.

"You're going to come so fucking hard on me," Jack gritted out as he stretched Paul's hole. Lissy wiggled restlessly.

When Jack's fingers moved in and out with ease, he added a third. The burn spread through Paul's body like wildfire. He focused on not coming, but with Jack strumming his prostate, it was damn near impossible.

He stilled. Lissy drew him down in a mind-blowing kiss, and Jack added more lube. When Paul's mind stopped whirling, his lover was burrowing into him. The fat head moved past his rim, and he held his breath. Jack's rasps of pleasure washed over his skin, feeding his desire for more. To feel all of him.

He released a long moan, and Jack echoed it. Jack eased in until he was firmly seated in him. Long and thick and so fucking good. Paul's mind did a slow revolution, processing pleasure-pain, need and passion.

"Damn, I want more," he forced through a clenched jaw. Jack groaned and pushed another millimeter deeper. Pressure built. Lissy squeezed his cock while Jack took him to new heights. This was how Jack must have felt in the hot tub the previous day. And soon Lissy would be in his place, taking each of them.

Paul couldn't move. Lissy and Jack bucked against him. Jack dug his fingers into Paul's hips, and Lissy raked her blunt nails over his shoulders.

He gave them the reins and let himself feel.

Lissy's breasts jiggled and her lips were bright red from their kisses. Her eyes darkened. Her body compressed him.

Then she was coming. Need rushed up, hot and fast. Paul tossed his head back and roared as his ass clamped down on Jack and the first hot spurts jetted from him. Jack pumped two more times, his orgasm heating Paul.

Nope, he'd never be the same.

* * * * *

"Rode hard," Paul said, diving into the mattress as if he'd been bucked off a bull.

"And put away wet," Lissy breathed, eyes closed and looking more content than Jack had ever seen her.

With a grunt Jack got up and disposed of the condom. When he caught his reflection in the bathroom mirror, he stopped and stared.

Who was this guy with the overly bright eyes? He'd just fucked his best friend. Paul had just given him the ultimate gift—his body and trust.

A lump formed in Jack's throat. He turned on the faucet and washed his hands then his face. When he returned to the bed, the pair was snuggled together. Jack stopped in his tracks.

They looked so right together. They *felt* so right to Jack. He was in no way prepared to let Lissy leave when her time was up. He wanted to start over again, get her onstage, win her over.

Somehow her presence had won him Paul too.

He approached the bed on soft feet and stood staring at them. Paul opened his eyes and extended a hand toward him. Grinning, Jack grasped it and crawled up behind him, fitting his body against Paul's hard one and entangling his fingers with Lissy's.

Their breathing fell into a rhythm. Outside the world went on, but in here Jack had true happiness. This felt different.

He mentally shook himself. No use in pondering what could be, because it wouldn't happen. Lissy would return to her life and he and Paul would have each other. They'd also have other women to share.

No.

Jack's denial was swift and powerful. He couldn't imagine anyone but Lissy lying here with them. Bungalow 3, 7, 9. Hell, he'd been in them all. But this was where he belonged.

The lump returned to his throat, burning. Was this how Riggs and Hugh had felt when they'd found Sybill?

Jack squeezed his eyes shut and focused on the pleasant haze of post-orgasm. Too bad his damned mind wouldn't shut up.

Chapter Eight

When Lissy was with Jack and Paul, time flew. Unfortunately. She wasn't ready to think about leaving the ranch let alone walk away from them.

She tried to let go of her school-girl obsession and focus on the time she had with them. They spent time nursing the calf, which did indeed have some birthing trauma the vet had originally overlooked. They were assured time would make the calf more limber.

They skinny-dipped in the pond and made a midnight run to the hot tub. Paul fed her sweet bites of Cook's award-winning peach cobbler, and Jack swiped a bottle of chocolate syrup from the kitchen and they took turns smearing it on each other.

And they rode horses. The guys guided her over every acre, teaching her the lay of the land. Very quickly she felt more at home here than she ever had in her hometown. She was a competition horsewoman, but until this week she'd never thought of herself as a cowgirl.

Wrapping her arms around herself, she gazed out over the ranch. The little red roofs in the valley below made her smile. When Jack rested a hand on her shoulder, tears flooded her eyes.

Stop. I'll just enjoy my time I have left and stuff down these feelings until I get home.

She was afraid of the aftermath of her trip. A week's worth of orgasms given by two stud men wasn't all she'd gotten from her vacation. She also had too much emotion for both of them as well as two new best friends.

Damn.

Drawing a deep breath, she turned into Jack's arms.

"Rodeo's tonight, sugar," Jack said with a kiss on her forehead.

Paul sidled up to the fence and leaned against it, grinning.

She pulled away a bit to look at him, then Paul. "What rodeo?"

"The Boot Knockers put on a rodeo. Paul here does some trick riding. Others rope and ride."

She studied Jack. "And what do you do?"

"I'm the clown."

She chuckled, and Paul nudged him in the shoulder. "You are not," she said.

"No, he is in a way." Paul's eyes sparkled with affection for Jack. "He gets the crowd fired up with a certain routine."

She looked between them. "You going to fill me in?"

"No, it's a surprise." Jack pinched her bottom—hard. "You'll see tonight. What do you want to do with your last day on the ranch?"

Her stomach hollowed, and her heart plummeted into the chasm. The tears that had surfaced a moment ago were back with an army of friends. She bit the inside of her lip to ward them off.

When she didn't answer, Paul threaded his fingers through her hair and lightly separated the strands. "What about a picnic?"

"Where?" Her heart hurt. Hell, what was she going to do tomorrow? She'd never be able to hold back her tears.

Jack stared into the distance. "I know the perfect place."

Paul rode down to the grub house and came back with a picnic basket slung over his arm while Lissy lay with her head in Jack's lap and he massaged her scalp and neck. She never wanted to move, but they ordered her onto

Polly's back and the three of them set off in the direction of the funnel of land where Lissy had first really fallen for Jack.

Her throat was tight the entire ride. Jack tried to make her race by galloping ahead, but she rode beside Paul at her own pace. Occasionally their thighs would brush as their horses got close.

"One of my favorite spots," Jack said, dismounting.

Paul followed and set the basket on the ground. When Lissy didn't move, he approached her. Concern shadowed his face. "You all right?"

"Yes, of course. This will be a perfect picnic spot."

Jack unrolled a blanket taken from his saddle pack, and Paul unloaded the contents of the basket. Chicken salad sandwiches, apples, small containers of macaroni salad and a packet of double-fudge cookies that looked divine.

Lissy's appetite had fled, though.

She accepted a sandwich from Paul but didn't bite into it. Turning her face up to the sky, she basked in the sun on her skin. "I'm going to miss Texas."

Jack drew a circle around her knee. Tingles shot up from his touch to settle in her pussy. "Going to miss this?" He walked his fingers right up to the V of her legs.

"Uh-huh." She met his gaze, shocked to find him sober. Could he be feeling the loss too?

She bit into her sandwich, and delicious flavors partied on her tongue. "I'm going to miss Cook's food. She even makes chicken salad taste gourmet."

"She's a treasure, for sure." Paul said "for sure" like "fo sho". Lissy smiled.

"She makes the best hangover shake too," Jack added, swiping his tongue over his lip to gather a crumb.

Lissy laughed. "How many times have you drunk a hangover shake?"

"More times than I care to admit. I'm done drinking though." He and Paul exchanged a look.

They ate in silence for a while, though it wasn't uncomfortable. The burning pain Lissy felt at leaving tomorrow didn't lessen, but she'd have to learn to live with it sooner or later.

Paul smacked his hands together to brush off the crumbs then he bit into an apple. Lissy squeaked as juice landed on her cheek. Before she could wipe it away, Jack's lips covered it.

His kiss was simple and filled her with pure happiness. Their time together had been much more than lust and sex-crazed romps. They'd formed a friendship she would forever value.

Paul pulled her feet into his lap and massaged her calf above her boot. Jack popped a piece of chocolate cookie into her mouth. As the decadent flavors melted on her tongue, she groaned.

Then she felt two hands working up her body and she gave herself up as lost.

* * * * *

Wild banjo music played through the loudspeakers surrounding the corral and bleachers. Women huddled together talking animatedly, but Lissy wasn't there. Where the hell was she?

Jack whacked his gloves together to remove the dust before putting them on. The heat was oppressive even though the rodeo started early in the day. Still, when you were wearing a denim shirt and leather chaps, it was too hot.

Even if you weren't wearing anything under the chaps.

Someone smacked his ass cheek—hard. Whirling, mouth open on a gasp, Jack came face-to-face with Paul.

Several cowboys nearby winked and smiled. After trying for so long to claim Paul, Jack felt like strutting. He leaned close and kissed the smirk right off Paul's face.

When he tensed, Jack waited for his lover to shove him away. They weren't exactly "out" in front of the other Boot Knockers. Shock tore through him as Paul dragged him to a secluded spot behind the stands. He pinned Jack to the wooden wall and braced his arms around him.

"It's official. The guys think you've lost your mind."

"Nah," Paul drawled. "They just think I finally gave in. They know about your amazing blowjob skills."

Jack laughed, but when he stared at Paul's lips, he grew serious. "What's going to happen when she leaves?"

He dipped his head so the brims of their hats bumped. "With us?"

"Yeah." Jack's insides quivered at the idea of going back to the old ways — pursuing Paul and aching for more. Yearning for a human tie.

He had it with both Paul and Lissy. Hell, even if Paul wanted him, how were they going to get on without her?

"I was an idiot to keep you at bay for so long." Paul's words burned with intensity and his eyes were icy fire. "You mean a helluva lot to me, Jack. I'm done playing games."

Jack's heart tumbled boots over spurs. Struggling to speak around his emotion, he said, "No exclusivity is written into our contracts."

"Fuck the contracts."

Holly's voice rang across the area as she took the microphone.

"Shit, they're introducing us. C'mon." Paul caught Jack's shoulder and towed him across the field. They took their positions in the long line of Boot Knockers. The women hooted and hollered.

Jack scanned the crowd. "Where's Lissy?"

Paul folded his arms over his chest. "You'll see."

Before Jack could ask what the hell was going on, Holly nudged him out of the line, made him turn to expose his bare ass in the chaps and walloped him with a riding crop.

The sting across his ass was a live wire, but the crowd erupted. He met Paul's laughing gaze. "Give 'em a good show, cowboy," he said with a wink.

Heart full, Jack ran into the center of the arena and took over entertaining the crowd. He only wished Lissy was here to see.

* * * * *

"Oh my God, my sides hurt from laughing." Lissy leaned against Paul, gasping for air as Jack did a series of handsprings.

Paul tucked her close to his side, cracking up over Jack's antics. "His routine always kills me."

Jack did a shimmy that made something down low shimmy too.

"I should be annoyed that all these women can see my cowboy's junk, but he's so funny I can't possibly be upset." Lissy wiped tears of mirth from her eyes.

Jack was unbuttoning his shirt nice and slow in a striptease that had the women going wild. Paul watched with a crooked smile. Lissy leaned onto tiptoe to kiss the bracket that appeared on his cheek.

"So the time you've spent with Jack—that wasn't only for me, was it?"

He focused on her, and a new kind of heat burned behind his eyes. "No. I guess he's been working on me for a long time and I've finally realized the reason I haven't been pushing him away."

She flattened a palm against his warm, broad chest. "He knows?"

Paul nodded. "Just told him a bit ago."

She didn't like the thought of leaving them, but at least they'd have each other. Maybe they'd talk about her sometimes.

Paul tugged her against his body, grinding the evidence of his arousal into her hip. When he whispered into her ear, her nipples hardened. "I wanted you so bad, Lissy. I thought I'd go crazy if I didn't get a chance at you."

"You're saying Jack saved you from going to the loony bin."

"Abso-fucking-lutely." He dragged out the word while nuzzling her ear. Heat licked her insides. Need mingled with a splash of sadness. Tomorrow was her last day with these two guys. She didn't want to think about the stabbing pains in her chest at the thought of leaving. Never seeing them again would feel like tearing off a limb—or two.

Dammit, tears threatened again.

Jack finished his routine with a gyration that sent the crowd into hysterics. Feet pounded the wooden bleachers, and the other Boot Knockers roared.

Paul pinched her chin between his fingers and turned her to look at him. "Knock 'em dead." With a smack on her ass, he sent her running. She cut across the field toward the horse that Hugh was holding for her. Planting her palms on its behind, she launched into the saddle.

Years of practice and a million sit-ups had given her enough muscle to perform that trick. Paul whooped and fist-punched the air as she took off into the arena.

Cowboys ran out with some hurdles for jumping, and she performed the leaps with ease. By the time she circled again, Jack was on the sideline, grinning at her. He doffed his hat as she passed, and she snagged it from his hands and placed it on her head.

It smelled of him.

God, how was she going to leave?

She leaned over her horse's neck and spurred him around to jump two hurdles in one long stride. The crowd cheered. But she only had eyes for the two guys standing on the side, their arms around each other.

A tear escaped, and she brushed it away.

* * * * *

"Fuck." Paul's voice sounded as if he'd gargled broken glass.

Jack looked at him hard. "What's wrong?"

"She's crying."

Jack looked closer at his gorgeous woman riding one of their best mounts. Sure enough, she was swiping at her eyes. Over and over.

"Dammit." He yanked off his chaps and grabbed his jeans. He tried to step into them without removing his boots and almost fell over.

"Dumbass." Paul's tone was affectionate but he didn't remove his gaze from Lissy as she executed perfect jumps.

In a flurry, Jack removed his boots and jumped into his jeans. He had to be careful zipping his fly because he hadn't bothered with underwear. By the time he had his boots back on, Lissy was flying out of the arena.

She brought the horse to a skidding stop and tossed Hugh the reins. Before she dismounted, Paul caught up to her. She twisted from his grasp. Jack's heart clenched at the sight.

Rushing forward, he blocked her path. "You can't go until we've talked," he said.

Her eyes streamed, and her throat worked against sobs. "Please move."

"Baby, please hear me out."

"I can't right now. I'm sorry." She shoved past, but had to skirt Hugh, Riggs and Sybill. She sidestepped around them, and continued on, arms hugged around her middle.

"What's going on here?" Hugh demanded, passing the reins to Jeremy.

Paul threw a look at Lissy's back. "There's something I need to tell you, Hugh."

"Oh fuck no."

Overhearing, Riggs pointed at his lover. "I told you something was brewing with these three."

"Son of a bitch." Hugh looked as if he might have a stroke. A vein ticked in his neck. Sybill grabbed his hand, but he didn't look away from Paul and Jack.

"I worked my ass off on this ranch for a lot of years. I wanted to become one of you more than anything, but I think my number is up." Paul's face was dead serious.

Jack braced his legs to keep from stumbling. "Holy fuck. Paul, what are you saying?"

"I don't know." He shook his head. "Dammit, yes I do. I wanted in Lissy's bed and I think I would have done anything to have a chance to be with her. She's..." He looked back at her. She was walking more slowly. Could she overhear them?

"I need to know more about her, and a week isn't enough. I'm requesting a leave."

"Whoa." Jack raised both hands, shock tearing through his system. "You aren't doing anything without me."

Hugh glared. He stabbed a finger at each man's chest. "You and you. In my office. Now."

Heart pounding, Jack hesitated. Hugh swept a hand toward the office building. "Let's go." Jack grasped Paul's arm and hauled him off as Lissy broke into a run. When he glanced over his shoulder, he thought his heart would be ripped from his chest.

Paul stared straight ahead as he walked.

Jack nudged him. "What the hell were you thinking, man?"

"We'll talk later." He followed Hugh's long strides to the office. Riggs came along, probably as a buffer between them and his lover.

The door slammed shut behind them, and Hugh stomped into his office. The others trailed in.

He whirled his leather chair and dropped into it as if he'd been shot. Jack gnawed his lower lip. They were in for it now. Hugh's wrath was no soft puff of air. Last time he'd been reprimanded for taking a practical joke too far, he'd felt like a five-year-old.

"Tell me what the fuck that was?" he asked slowly.

Paul spoke. "I'm willing to go without pay, as long as I get leave."

"Leave to do what?" Hugh's tone was deadly.

Jesus, was Paul really doing this? Jack's mind spun. His friend had lost his shit. He was throwing away his job?

When Jack thought about losing *Lissy*, it felt like a swift kick to the gut. He steeled his spine and stepped up to the desk.

"We'd like leave to explore our options."

Paul cut a look at him but didn't speak.

"We can expand our herd and look into buying more land from the adjoining ranch. I hear the owner's looking to sell."

"And?" Hugh arched a brow.

Jack stood so close to Paul that their bodies touched. He pushed out a breath. "And Lissy."

Hugh snorted. He flipped open a file and plucked a sheet from inside. Holding it up, he said, "You're going to give up your jobs for Larissa Lofton?"

"Yes." The instant Jack spoke the words, he knew it was the right course. The three of them went together like...like...

Well, he couldn't find the words but they needed time to explore this relationship.

"No leave," Hugh said. Riggs started in surprise, but Hugh rolled over his protest, "They're dropping like flies. You and I are out of circulation and we've barely recovered from losing Damian. What the hell is going on? We should start calling the ranch the Lovesick Puppies instead of Boot Knockers. Hell," Hugh said with a growl.

"You know what happened to us, Hugh. Don't discount what they're feeling. Jack and Paul have been moving this direction for a while. I've sensed it, and Paul confided a little to me. It doesn't come as a surprise, especially after Lissy got on that stage. I thought Jack would jump out of his skin to get to her."

"How are we going to replace them? Shit, it's *two cowboys*!"

"We have a few applications. We call them and get them in here next week."

Silence.

"Don't do this, man," Paul said.

"Hugh, can I speak with you alone?" Riggs's request got Hugh's attention. He waved toward the door, and Hugh reluctantly followed.

Paul met Jack's gaze. "We deserve this time together, the three of us."

Jack nodded. "She's really upset. She doesn't want to go, and dammit, I don't want to let her."

"What we had in that bungalow wasn't normal client/cowboy relationship stuff. She got to me. Here." He pressed his knuckles against his chest. "Just like you did months ago. It just took me a while to figure it out. I don't want to make the same mistake with Lissy."

"I know, man. We're on the same page with what we're feeling. If Hugh doesn't agree?" Jack asked.

Paul lifted a shoulder in a shrug. "Up until a few days ago I thought all I had was this ranch, but now I know differently. I have you and we both want Lissy."

Jack released a whoosh of air and clamped his arms around his best friend and lover. "We'll be okay. And Lissy —"

They could hear Riggs and Hugh arguing just outside the door but the words were muffled. Hugh's voice rose sharply and then it was silent. Paul swung his gaze toward Jack, his lips pressed into a tight line. Hugh wasn't going to let them take leave. A bead of sweat ran down Jack's temple, and he knuckled it away.

Hugh and Riggs entered. Hugh didn't bother resuming his seat behind the desk. He jerked a thumb at the open door. "Leave granted. Get out."

Jack's jaw dropped, but Paul was fast. He grabbed Jack's shoulder, and together they went to find their lover and tell her the good news.

* * * * *

Lissy rushed through the door of Bungalow 15 and slammed it behind her. She plastered her hands over it as if barricading anyone from entering.

On second thought—

She twisted the lock. She just needed a minute. A quiet minute to slow her racing heart and get hold of her emotions.

In all her years, she could count the number of times she'd cried. A lower leg fracture at eleven years old that kept her from competing in a huge state event. When her horse took a fall and was injured. When she missed an A on a test by half a lousy point.

All the moments seemed tame in comparison to this. Right now her heart was breaking.

She collapsed to the closest chair and lowered her face into her hands. Why now? It was just sex.

No, she couldn't even think that lie without wanting to pound her head against the wall. A few orgasms—though mind-blowing— weren't the reason she didn't want to leave the ranch.

All the moments that were about connections of the soul and not physical lust tethered her to the ranch. To Jack and Paul.

"I'm an idiot," she whispered. The low whir of ceiling fans was the only response.

She swiped the tears off her cheeks and went in search of a tissue. After blowing her nose, she felt more in control—at least until she spotted Jack's shirt draped over a chair.

Without thought she lifted it to her nose and sniffed. A shudder racked her.

Steeling herself against a total breakdown, she tried to ignore her heart and use her brain. This wasn't real. The whole vacation was an escape from real life. Women came to push their boundaries and find things they couldn't get in their daily lives.

If all of this was fantasy, she couldn't trust her instincts. Her emotions were in the way. When she entered a tricky jump, she flipped that emotional switch to the off position. The same had to happen here.

She'd leave the ranch and her cowboys behind. They'd go on with their jobs, caring for other women. Sharing other women.

Jealousy spiked, and she swallowed it like bile.

With determination, she went into the bedroom and located her suitcase. The few clothes she'd brought took minutes to pack. Her toiletries consisted of body wash, shampoo, sunscreen and lip balm.

She punched a button on her phone and spoke to the voice that responded. "Find closest cab company."

In moments a list and a map popped up on her screen. Getting away from the Boot Knockers Ranch was her only path. She couldn't face Jack and Paul again. She was like a wounded animal, and all she could think about was finding a hole. Getting away had been her only thought.

Oh God, this was too terrible.

She swiped her thumb over the screen, obliterating the numbers there just as someone pounded on the door, rattling it as though prepared to break it in.

Her heart hitched and she whirled.

"Lissy!"

* * * * *

"Why would she lock the door?" Jack brought his fist down on the wood—hard.

"If she has someone else in there, I'll break his legs." Paul hit it with his shoulder, shaking it loose in the frame.

"Just a minute!" Lissy called, a frantic edge to her voice.

Jack fell back, panting. Damn, what had begun as attraction had morphed into something too deep for words. Next week when the new group of women rolled in, he and Paul would not be in that auditorium selecting them. They'd be with Lissy, as long as she let them back in the bungalow.

She opened the door and he saw the traces of her emotion. "Baby..."

Dropping her gaze, she stepped aside. Jack's throat tightened and he reached for her. She drifted out of reach, but Paul pushed by him and tugged her into his arms. Jack shut the door, enclosing them all in the private space that had held more happiness for him than any other place in his life.

He and Paul had made the right decision.

Paul bracketed her face with his hands and dipped at the knees to stare into her eyes. She wouldn't look at him.

"Sweetheart, why are you upset?" Jack guided her long hair over her shoulder.

She shuddered. "I can't stay."

"That's okay, but we're free. We're coming with you," Jack said.

Her lips stretched into a grimace. "I can't let you do that. You belong here. What about your herd?"

Paul and Jack exchanged a look over her head. "You're right. We can't walk away from our animals," Paul said slowly. "That means you're staying with us."

She jerked free of Paul's hold and walked the whole way across the room. A big window seat ran the length of one short wall, but she didn't sit. She folded her arms and tried to look aloof when Jack knew she was aching inside.

The twist of her lips and the shadows in her eyes spoke loudly.

He took a step toward her, and she threw up her hands, warding him off.

"Look. This has been...fun."

"Just fun?" Paul's voice was gritty.

Blue eyes swimming with tears ticked from Paul to Jack, then slid away. "Amazing," she whispered. "But my life isn't here. If you're taking leave, use it to meet your own goals."

"Is that what you really want, Lissy? Everything is your choice, but judging by how upset you are, I think you're leaning toward our idea." Jack moved forward. "Our goal is to be with you for longer than one week. You can't deny this connection the three of us feel."

She shook her head. "It's not real. I mean, what you two have is. That's evident."

"Lissy." Paul stalked toward her. "What Jack and I have was brewing for a while, but you were some kind of catalyst that spurred me into action and drew us all together." He waved his hand between himself and Jack.

Swooping in, Jack caught her in his embrace. She locked her arms over her chest, feeling like a frightened bird in his hold. He tried to gentle her just like an animal. Placing his mouth to her ear, he crooned soothing words. "Shhh, baby. It's okay. Everything will be okay."

Paul wrapped his arms around both of them, his lips grazing her cheek then Jack's jaw. "Let us do this our way."

Hell, when Paul got bossy, Jack melted. If Lissy could stand up to him, she was a stronger woman than he'd first believed.

She held up her hands, warding them both off. "Just...give me a moment. I need some distance."

* * * * *

Lissy walked the whole way across the room and turned her back to the two big cowboys taking up too damn much space in her bungalow. They couldn't just barge in here and command that she give in to their whim of quitting their jobs and making her the filling of a cowboy sandwich forever.

What she'd set out to do, she'd achieved. No more virginity, an amazing weekend with not one beautiful god of a man, but two.

She had a life in California, and maybe next season she'd pair up with Melia for another go at gold for team Double L-M. She had her parents nearby, good friends and a career in equine science.

But she'd be miles and miles away from the four blue eyes that had captured her heart. She thought about giving them her cell number. Texting would keep them linked without all this...confusion.

Too easily she imagined the kinds of texts she could expect, though. Especially with Jack's sense of humor. Knowing they wanted her would just leave her craving more.

She felt their heavy gazes on her back and didn't know whether to scream or run into their arms. In the past few hours they'd made her laugh, groan, swept her off her feet and infuriated her.

Dammit to hell, she loved them, didn't she?

Turning to look at them from the corner of her eye, she said, "I don't understand what's going on with me. I'm not this kind of woman."

"You're a beautiful, smart and funny woman with a love of life most people don't have. You were bold enough to come to the ranch and take what you needed. Why won't you allow yourself to recognize that your needs have changed?" Jack stared into her eyes.

"I-I can't think straight."

A ghost of a grin brushed Paul's lips. "I couldn't either when Jack's advances started affecting me. Or later when I opened your file, sweetheart."

Her gaze flashed to his, and she read the truth in his eyes. He'd been through a gamut of emotions himself. He'd weathered through and made it to the other side.

She could too. She'd trusted him in so many ways — both of them. Maybe they could guide her through this too. She wanted to stay so badly.

"You're a bold woman, Lissy. Booking a trip like this isn't for the faint-hearted. You aren't going to back down from this challenge, are you? Run from your feelings?"

"We can see you want to stay," Jack added.

Looking between them, she felt her resolve crumbling. She could leave the ranch tomorrow and never see them again, or she could put her hands in theirs and make a go of a new sort of life.

Paul ducked his head to peer into her face. The line carved around his upturned lips snapped the last twigs of resistance. "Challenge accepted?"

Jack pressed near, invading her thoughts and awareness. He touched her fingers. "Say yes. Give us more time to explore what this could be."

Her words clogged her tight throat. They weren't demanding forever—just the time to figure out if their relationship could be more. Wasn't that what she wanted too? "I don't know how to say no. I don't *want* to say no."

Paul made a noise in his throat, and Jack closed in. They locked her between them, just holding her for long minutes. She wrapped her arms around each, accepting slow, deep kisses from them. When all three tongues collided, a shudder racked her.

Jack ran his hands over her back, down to the curve of her ass. When he squeezed the cheeks, dragging her against him, she sucked in a breath.

Paul explored her torso and down to the V between her legs. Writhing, she issued a harsh gasp.

Jack took off her top and then Paul divested her of her bra. He ducked his head and sucked her nipple into his mouth. Jack watched his lover's cheeks hollow as he gently pulled on her nipple.

Lissy groaned and stretched her fingers over Jack's skull as he took hold of the opposite nipple. She yanked him near, closing her eyes to savor the moment.

With each lash of his tongue around her nipple, he drew longer moans from her. When she started to quiver, he straightened. Paul tipped her against his chest and lifted her off her feet.

They moved to the bedroom.

"Gorgeous woman, you've sealed your fate. We're going to make you scream our names until you're hoarse." Paul loosed his belt buckle, and she wet her lips.

"I can't just stay in bed all day and night with you two. What will I do to stay busy here?" She followed Paul's movements and got distracted by the spattering of hair on Jack's strong forearms as he reached for his own belt buckle.

"Lots of horses on this ranch. I'm sure Hugh wouldn't mind paying to have a resident professional." Paul unzipped his fly. The grating noise of each tooth prickled Jack's skin.

Lissy's pulse raced. "I adore the ranch, and I'd love that. But what if Hugh doesn't want me on staff?"

Jack's eyes crinkled with amusement. "This is Texas, baby. Lots of horses and only a few country vets. You've seen for yourself how thin our vet, Ennis, is stretched."

"Baby, listen to me." Jack took her wrist and lifted her hand. Pressing her palm to his chest, he stared into her eyes. "We'll work it out. The feelings are all there. We just need more time to figure out how to make our lives fall into place."

Heart in her throat, she nodded. Tears didn't feel far away, but she was happier than she'd ever been. Reaching for each of them, she chose her path. "Come here. Both of you."

With a whoop of joy, Jack captured her mouth. He delved his tongue between her lips.

When Paul added his tongue, they all shared a groan. As Jack flickedhis tongue over Lissy's, then Paul's, the universe shifted into place. Lissy hauled them both closer and threw herself into the kiss.

Paul broke first. He stripped the rest of his clothes off in an instant. As he reached for Lissy's waistband, Jack undressed. By the time his boots hit the floor, Lissy was bare.

Her pussy was swollen and wet.

Jack stretched on the bed. Paul flipped her, positioning her so her ripe folds hovered over Jack's lips. Her breath rasped, sounding harsh.

Desperate need and love rose inside her. The ache between her legs needed to be satisfied, just as their desire for her to stay soothed her heart.

He ran his tongue up and down her seam, and her juices pooled on him. Small moans burst from her.

As she ground on his face, their hands were all over her, lighting her nerve endings on fire.

She looked up to see Paul rolling Jack's cock through his fist. When Lissy's movements grew jerkier, Jack doubled his efforts.

Bliss consumed her as he swirled his tongue around her bud again and again. They flipped her, spreading her wide to accommodate two heads.

She stopped breathing as they teased her together. For a brief second they tangled tongues in her opening. Then Paul was gone once more, licking a path toward her ass.

She rocked, her whole body taut. Pulsations met Jack's tongue. He worked over her slash until she quaked. Paul did something that made her cry out. Her whole body tensed.

Suddenly she was coming. Hard and fast— her fingers in Jack's hair and her entire body twitching with release.

Her connection with her men drove her to new heights. Waves pounded her and gritty moans escaped.

As Jack extended her pleasure, Paul left the bed. She'd barely gained her senses before Paul slipped a condom over Jack's erection. He grunted, mouthing Lissy's clit more softly.

Paul latched onto her waist and pulled her off Jack. "Sit on his cock, baby."

She slid down his body and impaled herself on Jack. When he pulled her into a kiss, emotion lay salty on her tongue. He stroked her cheek, and she couldn't hold back. She hurled himself into showing him just how strongly she felt for him.

She gasped, and he tore his mouth away, holding her gaze as Paul probed her ass.

"Just one finger, baby," he said.

Paul's nerves snapped as he watched his lover disappear into Lissy's tight body. He stretched her with one finger, then two. He bit off a growl.

He had to slow down and make this good for her. She would need to be gentled into taking him in her ass, and the fullness of having them both —

His breathing grew ragged as he added a third finger, spreading them to ease his way. She moaned more. Jack's face was red with the exertion of holding back.

"Think you can take my cock?" he whispered to her.

"Mmm-hmm."

Jack issued a primal grunt.

Removing his fingers, Paul squeezed ample lube onto his stiff, condom-covered cock. He wanted this to be ultra-pleasurable for Lissy, and easing his path would help.

Holding his erection at the base, he pushed it into her opening. Pulsing against the tight rim at first, then sinking slowly. A little more each time, until he was halfway in.

"Shit, I can feel you," Jack said raggedly.

"Oh myyyy," Lissy moaned.

"A little more." Paul's head swam with the need to pound into her — now. But her comfort came first. He wiggled his hips, burrowing deeper. Squeezing his eyes shut, he continued to sink into her body. When he was seated fully in her, they all fell still.

Lissy's breathing grew erratic. It grew louder until she burst out, "Move!"

They did. He and Jack moved in tandem, fucking in and out, stretching her to full capacity. The heat in Paul's body mounted, but the pressure in his chest was greater. Dammit, he could barely remember a time he didn't have Jack and Lissy as lovers.

His throat slammed shut on a roar. As he ground into her ass, he fought for control, but Jack's cock sliding against his coupled with Lissy's tightness was stealing all thought.

Her body convulsed around him. Jack's eyes were wide and glassy, fixed on some distant point. Paul found Jack's fingers. Meshing them, he gripped Lissy's hip and let himself go.

When her contractions hit, Paul was unprepared. With a grunt, liquid heat rushed up. He pushed deeper as his orgasm slammed him. Jack stiffened, a vein pulsed in his throat and he opened his mouth wide.

Lissy jerked between them as they rode their orgasms. Her low, keening noises pushed Paul on. When the pressure in his groin fled, he met Jack's glossy gaze. Yeah, he wasn't ashamed to admit his feelings for his best friend. Jack had taught him life was too short to let it slip by, which was why he'd owned his feelings for Lissy and Jack in front of Hugh and his colleagues.

His new lifestyle fit him so perfectly, he couldn't figure out what had stopped him before.

Collapsing forward, he trailed kisses over her spine. Perspiration clung to her golden skin. Jack gripped Paul's fingers. Emotion clogging his throat, he squeezed them back. Then Lissy found their linked hands and Paul knew everything would be all right.

Chapter Nine

"The air's cooler up here, I swear." Despite his words, sweat streamed off Paul's chest.

Jack grunted agreement while pounding a tent stake into the ground. They'd purchased the roomiest tent possible. Erecting it on the ridge a short distance from the herd seemed like a good idea until Lissy realized they were a long distance from indoor plumbing.

She sat back on her heels and watched her men. "I don't know if this is going to work."

They both looked up at her, worry creasing their brows. She almost giggled then caught herself.

"I mean, I'm outdoorsy. But I'm no primitive woman. I like hot water and bathrooms."

"It's only for a week or so. And we can go down to the ranch at any moment," Paul assured her, stretching a line between the rain fly of the tent and another stake. Jack pounded it into the ground.

She looked between them. "Only a week? What happens in a week?"

A boyish grin claimed Jack's handsome face. His eyes sparkled. "We bought a travel trailer. A guy's hauling it up as soon as possible."

She sank to the ground with her legs crossed and processed this information. It had only been days since she'd agreed to stay on the ranch, and it was taking some getting used to. First, the freedom of knowing they chose her even when she wasn't paying. Plus giving up her life, if only for a short time, was an adjustment.

"The trailer will have a flushable toilet and we'll fill the water tank every day." Paul shot her a wink that sent ribbons of heat through her body.

Jack tipped his head, eyes faraway. "Are those hooves I hear?"

Paul stilled, but right away Lissy said, "Yes."

She stood as the guys gained their feet. A rider came over the ridge — then another.

Lissy's heart tumbled as she recognized Hugh and Riggs. Without thinking she edged close to her cowboys. They each took a hand, linking all three in the face of whatever problems had come knocking.

Hugh dismounted and Riggs did too. The horses immediately began cropping grass.

"Your animals are eating our yard." Jack's attempt at a joke fell flat.

"What's going on?" Paul asked.

Lissy looked between the guys. She was usually good at reading people, but with these rough cowboys she was out of her element. She had a lot to learn.

"Well, besides the fact that Ty has no right eyebrow? We have a sick horse and we need Lissy." Hugh's gaze penetrated her.

Belly quivering, she nodded. "Of course I'll come."

"Wait—what happened to Ty's eyebrow?" Paul asked.

"That practical joke the guys planned got out of hand. They tried to wax his chest and"— waving a hand, he looked at Lissy—"other things. Somehow his eyebrow got it."

Riggs snorted a laugh. "He looks possessed."

"We'll all ride down," Jack said, brushing his thumb over her palm reassuringly.

Hugh gave a short nod. "That's a good idea. We have some updated contracts for you to sign. All of you." His gaze skipped from Paul to Lissy to Jack.

"What's this about?" Paul stepped forward as if ready to fight. Riggs tensed, and Lissy's belly flipped over.

She'd lived with women her entire life and had no idea how these guys would operate. Would they pound each other until an agreement was formed? Hell, she didn't know what was even going on.

"We'll explain later. Just come down to the office." With that, Hugh swung back into the saddle. Riggs lingered another second, giving them a small smile.

When they rode out of the camp, Lissy stared at her lovers. Apprehension was a tight fist in her chest.

"Whatever happens, we have our wits and hands. We can make a living anywhere," Jack said.

"That's right. And we have each other," Paul added.

As they abandoned the tent and mounted up for their ride to the valley, Lissy's nerves jangled. If not for her, the guys wouldn't be in this situation. But she couldn't deny her growing feelings or ignore the looks they gave each other or her.

Entering the office, she welcomed the cooler air while wishing like crazy she was back on that ridge.

Hugh was seated behind his desk and Riggs straddled a folding chair at the side. The seating before the desk was vacant. Hugh pointed, and the guys sat. Jack pulled Lissy onto his thigh, and Paul took her hand.

Linked — always linked.

She pushed out the breath she'd been holding.

"We've been thinking," Riggs said when Hugh didn't speak.

"Yes, we have. Your animals need prime grazing land, and our horses don't need nearly as much as they have. We're transferring some to you." Hugh pushed a paper toward Paul.

With a shock, Lissy realized it was a deed.

"Holy shit," Jack said. Riggs chuckled and toggled the toothpick in the corner of his mouth with a forefinger.

Paul didn't speak for a long minute. Finally he asked, "Why?"

Hugh leaned back in his chair and looked between them. "Beef's a good investment. You give us seven percent annually until the land is paid for."

Jack stared at the deed and let out a low whistle. "With this much land, we can put a lot more cows on it."

"Cattle is a solid future for the ranch. You two have covered the start-up costs with your own wages. Riggs and I pay for our own horses. In the end, the guys all make money because they all own a chunk of the land where our animals are raised."

"What's this about contracts?" Paul leaned forward in his chair, his hand still pinned to the deed.

Hugh shifted some papers again. "We figured it was good to put everything in writing." He passed out three sheets.

Lissy accepted hers, pulse racing. When she skimmed the first words, her mouth fell open. "This is a contract making me caregiver to your horses."

Jack and Paul both looked at her then back at their papers. Jack whistled through his teeth. "Does this mean what I think it does?"

Riggs grinned and Hugh nodded. "That's right. If any of you choose to change your minds, the contracts will be dissolved immediately."

"If you decide to go back to the bungalows," Riggs said with a knowing smirk.

Hugh tossed out a pen. "Read and sign. Then the land is yours to put more cows on. Lissy, we only ask that you come to the valley to check out the horses daily. If anything is wrong, you'd be expected to care for the animal. That might mean staying on the ranch for a spell until the horse is recovered."

"We'd provide you with lodging of course," Riggs said.

"Not in the bunkhouse," Jack ground out, locking her more securely to his lap.

"Of course not. We have a guest room in our house. She'd stay with us."

She met Hugh's gaze and they shared a smile.

She couldn't believe this was happening. As she reached for the pen, a weight lifted from her. After her whirlwind decision to stay, the winds were calming. She was no longer a tumbleweed blowing wildly. This contract was exactly what she'd needed, and judging by the expression on Hugh's face, he knew that.

She put pen to paper and wrote her name neatly. "I'll take the job, and thank you."

"You can see the payment terms in section two."

"Yes, they're fine." She couldn't keep the excitement from seeping into her tone.

Jack's smile spread and Paul's followed. She handed Jack the pen and he signed. Paul finished too and pushed all three sheets back to Hugh. He put them away without a glance.

When he stood, they all gained their feet. Paul bounced on his toes as if eager to embark on their new adventure. "Thank you for the opportunity." He stuck out a hand and Hugh accepted it with a hard clasp.

Jack shook Riggs's hand, and then they switched. Lissy met Hugh's gaze as he gripped her hand. "Welcome to the new chapter of your lives."

"What made you change your mind?" Paul asked.

Hugh grinned. "I recognize a lost cause when I see it. Now get outta here."

So giddy she didn't know if she could make it outside let alone onto horseback, Lissy left the office with her cowboys. As soon as they were outside, Jack released a whoop that made the horses skittish.

Paul threw his arms around her, and Jack leaped at them. They grappled in a dance. Laughing, Lissy planted a kiss on both sets of lips.

"I never expected that." Paul's eyes gleamed.

"Me either. Let's get the hell out of here before he changes his mind." Grinning from ear to ear, Jack swung into the saddle.

Lissy and Paul gained control of their mounts, and all three set off across the field toward the ridge. How she'd ended up so lucky was beyond her, but she'd grab hold of the reins of life and hold on tight.

The big Texas sky was dotted with puffs of cloud and the scent of crushed grass filled Lissy's head. Joy broke over her, and she kicked her horse in the sides. Throwing a look back at her lovers, she called, "Race ya!"

And took off in pursuit of her new life.

THE END

Read on for a peek at ROPIN' HEARTS, Book 4 of The Boot Knockers Ranch series

Bree sized up the fence. As far as she could tell, it wasn't electric, so no one would find a crispy piece of Bree bacon on the forbidden boundary between the Roberts land and the Boot Knockers Ranch.

Sinking into a crouch, she extended one leg and eased it under the lowest wire strand. Then she flattened herself on the ground and shimmied over to the "dark side". A thrill hit her belly as she rolled under, at least until a sharp pain speared her scalp.

Crying out, she clapped a hand over the spot. Dammit, her hair was caught on the barbed wire. She carefully tugged the strands free while keeping an ear out for anyone who might discover her on the neighboring ranch. The guys on Daddy's ranch had been warned by her father to haul her butt back if they spied her on the Boot Knockers land.

What Daddy doesn't know won't hurt him.

Freed, she jumped up and brushed the grass off her slim, red tank top and the tiniest cutoffs she owned. When she wore them on the ranch, the cowboys gaped at her. Sure, she liked the attention, but the ranch hands weren't for her. Also, those men were *real* crusty cowboys. Not at all like the Boot Knockers who only pretended to be cowboys.

Those were fine gods of men — muscled, tanned, some tattooed. She'd stared at the brochure with their pictures so long she felt she knew every man. Some wore the lines of squinting into the sun; others had boyish faces that didn't look mature enough to do the job.

The Boot Knockers Ranch didn't deal in cattle. Sure, they dabbled in beef, and word was they had some horse stock too, but Bree knew what they really did.

They treated ladies to toe-curling sex therapy. From what she'd read in the brochure, women with hang-ups over body image or traumatic sex experiences could pay for a week on the ranch and a gorgeous Boot Knocker would take care of her.

Bree's nipples peaked under her tank top as she walked the ridgeline toward the main buildings in the distant valley below. She'd been trying since she was sixteen to get brave enough to crawl under that fence. Years later, she was determined to see the Boot Knockers Ranch for herself.

One small problem faced her — she hadn't paid to be there. She brushed her long hair off her face. It wouldn't matter that she didn't have the huge fee or that she'd never make that much money waitressing in her entire life. Her short-shorts were her entry fee.

As she descended the slope, she surveyed the land. A few people were walking between the wooden cabins with red roofs. She figured no one would look twice at a woman on their land, especially with her legs.

She was aware of the lean, curvy lines developed by years of trick riding. She'd also done the rodeo-queen gig for a couple years and had a second-place trophy. Her daddy said he was mighty proud of her, but she didn't like being second.

She got a closer look at the ranch — huge barns, a chicken coop and cabins were self-explanatory. But what were those two vast metal buildings used for?

Tingles rode up and down her spine. She'd soon find out.

She passed the largest barn and circled to the closest building. As she reached the door, her heart jerked against her ribs. She drew two deep breaths before gripping the handle and pulling it wide.

Poking her head in, she found a dining hall. Long tables ran the length of the room, with a few intimate seating groups against the wall of windows. A buffet was set up.

Hell, it looked like one of the resorts in Cancún where she'd been on spring break her second year of college.

Thank God Daddy didn't know about half the things she'd done on that trip.

The room was empty, so Bree backed out and let the door close. Sun beat down and perspiration broke out on her forehead. Damn, she didn't want to face pseudocowboy sex gods with makeup streaming down her face. She paused to pat some of the dampness away, wiping her hands on her scrap of denim shorts.

A cry erupted, echoing on the light breeze blowing through the valley. She went on high alert. Several voices joined in another cry, and she set off toward the sound.

She rounded the second building, not bothering to look inside, and drew up short. Heart racing, hands clammy, she faced the most awesome sight ever. Tanned flesh glistening in the sun, muscles bunching and releasing. Cowboy hats askew, denim riding low on more than a dozen sexy hips.

Sure, there were females among the men, but Bree didn't give them a glance as she strode right into their midst. When she passed one tall cowboy with sandy hair flopping over one eye, she slowed. His face was clean-shaven, and his gaze dipped over her legs.

"Howdy," she said, putting more sway in her step.

He gave a low whistle that raised all the hairs on her body. Her insides melted, and her hips swayed for another reason.

Damn, would he come after her? Push her against one of those shade trees and kiss her like she needed to be kissed?

A knot of men separated, giving her a clear view of the reason they were gathered here. A Cornhole tournament. As she looked on, one gorgeous specimen with back muscles rippling grabbed a sack filled with corn and tossed it. The sack bounced off the rim of the wooden target but didn't go in the hole.

A cheer went up, and the stud threw his hat down. Bree skidded to a stop.

"That ain't a piece of clothing. Take something *off*, Stowe," one guy hollered.

Bree looked between them, shocked to see the men in states of undress. Some still wore plaid shirts rolled over thick forearms. Most wore jeans, but one guy had on only boots and a pair of navy boxer shorts printed with red lips.

She focused on the front of those boxers, wishing they were tight enough to see if rumors about the Boot Knockers were true — that they were all hung like horses.

Unable to see anything, she drifted close to a man with folded arms, his biceps bulky around a carved chest. She showed off one leg in the pose she'd snagged several guys with in college. Who cared about agricultural studies when she could major in men?

Insecurity prickled in the back of her mind. God, she hoped it worked this time. For all the webs she'd cast and guys she'd snared, she'd only had a handful of sex experiences. It was like guys were incapable of following through. And those who did hadn't lived up to her fantasies. None of them turned her crank.

Which is why I'm here.

"Nice tattoo," she said to him.

He looked up, a half smile creating a dimple smack-dab in the middle of one cheek.

His eyes were warm, dark hair plastered to his forehead. Slowly he held out one arm, palm up. She eyed his palm, wondering about the relationship between hands and cocks.

The tattoo of a belt buckle had writing she had to lean closer to read. "You're a rodeo guy?"

"Six years on the backs of bulls. Made good enough scores to go professional for a spell." His drawl wasn't Texan, but, whooooeee, did it make her sizzle.

"What's your name? I bet I know you."

"Elliot James. You follow the tour?"

"Yep. Did a bit of rodeoing myself." She caught the chain around her neck, tugging until the gold pendant rose from the depths of her cleavage. Oh yeah, Elliot was watching.

He hovered over her, bringing the spicy scent of man she craved so much. He pinched the pendant between two thick fingers, and her pussy flooded with thoughts of him pushing those fingers inside her.

Breathing heavily, she tried to control her reaction. She wanted to play it cool, but it was nearly impossible. Between his muscles and those dark, snapping eyes...

His breath washed over her, and her nipples hardened almost painfully. "Trick rider, eh? Bet you've got some tricks you could show me." He pitched his voice low.

Another cheer sounded, and she looked around to see a Boot Knocker unbuckling his pants with quick, practiced movements. When his tighty-whiteys came into view, his bulging erection was unmistakable.

"Nice wood," one guy called to him. "Marcie thinks so too. Care to meet us in Bungalow 2 after the tournament?" The cowboy who'd drawled this had his arm around a petite brunette who blushed an alarming shade of red.

Bree felt her own face grow warm, but parts much lower grew warmer.

Elliot let the pendant fall between her breasts once more, his gaze following its descent. "Who's your Boot Knocker?"

Panic lifted in her, a wild bird in her chest. She fought to control her voice. "Oh, him." She pointed in the direction of the group, hoping it was enough to trick Elliot.

"Ty?"

"Yes, that's right."

"I'll have to have a word about getting some trick-riding lessons from his girl, then."

"Sure." The word wobbled, and a constant throb took up residence between her thighs.

"Hey, Ty!"

Bree's muscles bunched, her body preparing to bolt without a command from her brain. This guy Ty would rat her out, and they'd surely know she didn't belong here.

Think. Think. Shit.

The gorgeous man had enough swagger to knock the air from her. She watched his muscles rolling, arms swinging loose, denim pulling tight over his thighs. Six-pack, hell. Ty looked as if he had twice that.

He let his gaze travel over her body, making her quiver with excitement. He was one of the baby-faced guys, but he was hot as hell. Besides, if he sprouted a five o'clock shadow, he'd look rough and dangerous enough to suit her.

She shifted her hips, giving him the best view of her toned thigh muscle. What was she doing? She should run for it.

Daddy always said I did tempt fate. We'll see if these two men make me the filling of a Boot Knocker sandwich.

Judging by the looks on Ty's and Elliot's faces, she was in a double-good position to get her dreams fulfilled.

"S'up, Elliot?" Ty's gaze didn't leave her. In fact, it sank to her breasts then up to her face.

"Your gal here is in to trick riding, and I feel the sudden need to learn. You up for sharing her?"

Bree's heart rate spiked. Her panties flooded.

"My gal…" Ty drawled the words, and her stomach hatched a thousand butterflies.

Run for it.

No, wait it out. If I can get two for the price of one pair of short-shorts…

Ty's eyes narrowed, and his long brows punctuated his suspicion. He swaggered near and snaked an arm around her middle. When he hauled her against his rock-hard body, she felt the tension running off him.

No escape. Shoulda run.

"Not with this one, Elliot. She's all talk in bed."

She sucked in a gasp. Confusion crossed Elliot's rugged features.

Ty delivered a pinch to her backside that made her yip. "For all her shorty-shorts, she's a cold fish. But I'll meet *you* in the bunkhouse at nightfall if you want to play."

With that, Ty started dragging her away. She dug in her bootheels.

"If you don't walk away with me normal, I'll pick you up and throw you over my shoulder, *Miss Roberts*."

Ice filled her veins. He knew her. How? Was there a wanted poster on the wall somewhere? This man saw dozens of women a week—surely he wouldn't remember her face after visiting her ranch.

"Let go of me!"

"I don't think so, sugar tits. You're trespassing. Wonder what *Daddy* would think of you down here getting corrupted."

"Sugar tits! Did you really just call me that?"

He placed his mouth close to her ear, heating it with his words. "Don't you want to be objectified, sweetheart? Isn't that why you're here?"

"No." She aimed a kick at his shin, but he moved his leg at the same moment. "Where are you taking me?"

Her pulse thrummed. For the first time since rolling under that fence, fear took hold. Not because Ty would likely hand her back to her father and she'd be in for the lecture of her life, but because she might not get another chance with a Boot Knocker.

No, I'll get a chance.

This time her bootheel glanced off Ty's shin. He didn't even flinch, just kept walking.

"What do you have — iron shins?"

He eyed her. "I've got iron *everything*, sweetheart. Now I'm going to put you into my truck and take you home." With him being shirtless, she was well aware of how hard he was.

"How do you know I didn't pay to be here?"

He glared at her. Up close his eyes were green, glowing like sea glass. She shut her jaw with such force her teeth grazed her tongue. Biting off a curse, she let him drag her another ten feet before really digging in.

She tore away and set her hands on her hips. "I can go on my own."

"I'd prefer to escort you." He didn't look fazed by her anger. She felt it simmering just below her skin, about to boil over if he tried to manhandle her again.

She waved a hand as if he were an annoying fly. "Go on back to your Cornhole."

He ran a hand over his chest and abs. She stopped breathing. The sight of long fingers over ridges of manscaped flesh rendered her panties a soggy scrap.

Sure, Ty had one of those crooked cowboy smiles.

Too bad he was an insufferable jerk.

After his treatment of her, she wouldn't have sex with Ty if he were the last Boot Knocker on earth.

Em Petrova

Em Petrova was raised by hippies in the wilds of Pennsylvania but told her parents at the age of four she wanted to be a gypsy when she grew up. She has a soft spot for babies, puppies and 90s Grunge music and believes in Bigfoot and aliens. She started writing at the age of twelve and prides herself on making her characters larger than life and her sex scenes hotter than hot.

She burst into the world of publishing in 2010 after having five beautiful bambinos and figuring they were old enough to get their own snacks while she pounds away at the keys. In her not-so-spare time, she is fur-mommy to a Labradoodle named Daisy Hasselhoff and works as editor with USA Today and New York Times bestselling authors.

Find Em Petrova at http://empetrova.com

DOUBLE DIPPIN'
LICKS AND PROMISES
A COWBOY FOR CHRISTMAS
LIPSTICK 'N LEAD

The Dalton Boys
COWBOY CRAZY Hank's story
COWBOY BARGAIN Cash's story
COWBOY CRUSHIN' Witt's story
COWBOY SECRET Beck's story
COWBOY RUSH Kade's Story

Single Titles and Boxes
STRANDED AND STRADDLED
LASSO MY HEART
SINFUL HEARTS
BLOWN DOWN
FALLEN
FEVERED HEARTS
DIRTY HAIR PULLER

Firehouse 5 Series
ONE FIERY NIGHT
CONTROLLED BURN
SMOLDERING HEARTS

The Quick and the Hot Series
DALLAS NIGHTS
SLICK RIDER
SPURRED ON

Also, look for traditionally published works on her website.

65817075R00192

Made in the USA
Middletown, DE
04 March 2018